W9-ACE-905

Mimi

John Newman

CANDLEWICK PRESS

This is a work of fiction. Names, characters, places, and incidents are either products of the author's imagination or, if real, are used fictitiously.

First U.S. edition 2011

Library of Congress Cataloging-in-Publication Data

Newman, John (John Stephen).
Mimi / John Newman. — 1st U.S. ed.
p. cm.
Summary: Mimi is determined not to give up on anyone or anything, but since Mammy died, her father never smiles, her sister Sally is in a bad mood, brother Conor keeps to himself, and even Sparkler the dog does not want to go for walks.
ISBN 978-0-7636-5415-3
[1. Grief—Fiction. 2. Single-parent families—Fiction.
3. Brothers and sisters—Fiction.
4. Family life—Ireland—Fiction.] I. Title.
PZ7.N47986Mim 2011
[Fic]—dc22 2010040147

11 12 13 14 15 16 RRC 10 9 8 7 6 5 4 3 2 1

Printed in Crawfordsville, IN, U.S.A.
This book was typeset in Slimbach.

Candlewick Press
99 Dover Street
Somerville, Massachusetts 02144

visit us at www.candlewick.com

For Astrid,

with love

Part 1

Chapter 1

Monday — 149 days since Mammy died

Monday is Granny's day. That's where I go after school every Monday. But first I always visit Mrs. Lemon's shop, to buy a candy bar with the rest of my lunch money, and Mrs. Lemon always says, "And what can I do for my good friend Miss Mimi today?"

"I'd like a Spiff bar, please, Mrs. Lemon."

"One Spiff bar coming up, young lady . . . and a few sweeties just for you."

And I hold out my hand, and Mrs. Lemon puts three or four sweets from the Pick 'n' Mix onto my palm and then she closes my fingers into a fist over them. Mrs. Lemon has been giving me free sweets every day since Mammy died.

So every day I make sure to drop into her shop. So does Sally, my big sister. She gets sweets too, but today Sally is late because she's hanging around with her Goth friends. Which means I get to Granny's first.

"Well! If it isn't young Mimi herself visiting her ancient grandparents," declares Grandad when he opens the door, as if it is a big surprise seeing me on the doorstep.

"It's Monday, Grandad," I tell him. "I come every Monday."

"Well, blow me down, so you do!" And he slaps his forehead with his hand as if to say how could he have forgotten. He does that every week.

And every week Granny comes bustling out of the kitchen, wiping her floury hands on her apron, and scolds him. "Well, are you going to let the poor child stand there all day? Come in, Mimi—don't mind the old fool."

Of course, Grandad is not really an old fool—well, he is old, but he's not a fool. Anyway, he doesn't mind Granny at all; he just laughs at her and winks at me.

Today Granny has made chocolate éclairs for me, and for Sally when she turns up, and for Conor (he's my big brother, but he has soccer on Mondays so he doesn't get here till later). Every Monday Granny cooks cakes — and that's why she's so fat, says Grandad.

"I am not!" she says in her pretend-to-be-cross voice. "Now sit down there, Mimi, and I'm going to pour you a big mug of hot chocolate to go with those chocolate éclairs!" So I sit at the table pushed up against the wall, and Granny puts on the red check tablecloth and the plate with the purple flowers on it and six fresh chocolate éclairs oozing with cream. Grandad reaches for one straightaway, but Granny slaps his hand. "Ladies first!" she tells him.

"Thank you, Granny," I say as she puts one on my plate first and on her plate second, and I smile in a ha-ha way at Grandad, who puts on his poor-me look.

"Now you may have one," Granny tells him as if he was a naughty little boy.

Sally arrives just as I have finished my second éclair. "I hope you've left some for me, you greedy pig," she says, and starts stuffing one into her mouth without even putting it on a plate. The cream squashes up her nose, but Granny just laughs.

"Who's the pig?" I ask her, but then Grandad drags me away to teach me chess and we leave Sally and Granny alone to have one of their big boring chats.

* * *

This is my second chess lesson. My first lesson was last Monday and it lasted about twenty seconds because I had to watch my favorite soap opera, *Southsiders*. I always have to watch *Southsiders* so that I can fill in Aunt M. on the episodes that she misses.

"Now we have ten minutes today before your rubbish show starts," says Grandad, spilling out the chess pieces. "So let's get cracking."

"It's not rubbish, Grandad—it's educational."

"Educational my bottom! Now, what's this piece called?" He holds up this little black upside-down cone.

Luckily I know this one. "It's a prawn, Grandad," I tell him confidently.

He laughs—that's how I know I've got it wrong. "No, not a prawn, Mimi, a PAWN."

"Prawn, pawn, what's the difference!" Sometimes, I find, adults fuss about nothing.

"One is a shellfish and one is a chess piece—that's the difference."

"I think my show is going to start, Grandad," I say. I don't think chess is going to be my game, somehow. I reach for the remote—but Grandad grabs it first.

"Not so quick, young lady." He holds up another black piece. This one looks like a horse's head. "Now, this piece is a knight."

"Then this must be a day," I say, holding up the white horse's head.

"What?" says Grandad, looking really puzzled.

"If the black one is night, the white one must be day," I explain.

Grandad just slaps his forehead with his hand and groans. "*Knight,* not *night*!" he says, which makes no sense to me. Then he sees that I'm only messing and sighs. "Oh, you! OK then, let's watch *Southsiders*." He ruffles my hair and we settle back on the couch to watch the TV.

Grandad wants to teach me chess because I'm Chinese and the Chinese invented chess about a million years ago, apparently. Personally I don't know what anyone sees in the game, but I don't tell him that.

Soon Grandad is snoring and I'm sucking my thumb and watching telly, and everything feels nice and comfy and peaceful and I wish I could stay there all evening, but at six o'clock we have to go home.

It is not a long drive home. Granny and Sally and I squash into the backseat of the jalopy, and Conor sits up in the front. Granny always tells Conor to get in the front because of his long legs, but he tells her that it is only because she is afraid to sit in the front when Grandad is driving.

"You could be right, Conor," Granny said, laughing. "Keep your eyes on the road, old man!" she tells Grandad.

"Are you driving the jalopy or am I?" asks Grandad as he drives through red lights.

"Those lights were red!" yells Granny. "Are you trying to kill us all?"

All my aunts say that Grandad shouldn't be driving anymore, but none of them has been brave enough to tell him yet. I hope they don't, because it would really upset him. Anyway, he hasn't had a crash yet, and when he drives he goes as slow as a snail.

Before we get back, Sally has to be dropped off at her weirdo friend Tara's house, which is good because I want to read her diary before she comes home.

Chapter 2

The house is dark when we get home, and chilly. Dad is fast asleep on the couch. He hasn't shaved again and his hair is all rumpled. I can see his toe sticking out of his sock. He looks so tired and sad and old that I don't wake him up. Anyway, Conor will soon enough when he gets started on his drums.

As usual Conor disappears into his bedroom and I turn on all the lights in the house before I slip into Sally's bedroom and lift up her mattress and pull out her diary. It is a lovely, heavy, hardback diary with little pictures of wildflowers on each page. Sally has a great collection of stationery in her room—markers of every color, folders and notebooks of all sizes, glue, tape, staples, paper clips, sharpeners, erasers, thumb-tacks, pens, pencils in all colors, and paper in all sizes and colors. She has cards and letter-writing paper that is scented with perfume and a little booklet of stamps — all neatly arranged on her desk.

But best of all is her diary. I love sitting on her bed and opening its heavy cover — very carefully so as not to mark the pages — and then I read her most private thoughts before I put it away exactly as I found it. She would kill me if she ever found out that I have read it.

I know I should not read Sally's diary, but I can't help myself. She hardly ever talks to me now since Mammy died, and it seems as if she doesn't care about anything or anybody anymore except her horrible friends with their black clothes and black lipstick and black mascara and black earrings and black moods.

But I know she does care, because she tells her diary everything. Well, almost everything. She tells her diary about how much her tummy aches when she thinks of Mammy and how she misses her hugs and even her scolding. She tells her diary that she misses our daddy now that he is so sad and tired all the time. She tells her diary that she loves her little sister, Mimi, even if she drives her crazy half the time, and how she wishes Conor wouldn't spend every minute playing the drums in his bedroom. She tells her diary how much she hates pizza now.

She tells her diary that she cries herself to sleep every night—just like I do. She tells her diary that sometimes she gets really cross with Mammy for getting herself killed on her bike and she hates feeling like that but she can't help it, and I know just what she means. You see I can't help it, either—so I have to read Sally's diary whenever I get the chance.

Also, my teacher, Ms. Addle, says that she wants the children in her class to read everything they can get their hands on—newspapers, comics, the backs of cereal boxes, the ads on the bus stop, signposts . . . everything we see. She didn't actually mention diaries but I bet she would have if she had thought of it.

But the most important reason I have to read Sally's diary is to find out what her dark and dreadful secret is.

Sally often mentions her "dark and dreadful secret" to her diary, but she never says what it is exactly, except that it is shameful and dangerous. But yesterday Sally told her diary that she would tell the terrible secret to it soon, so you can understand how excited I am as I sit on her bed with her diary on my lap.

I'll straighten out the bedcovers before I leave—I am very careful to cover all my tracks, like a good burglar. I open the diary to the new page, and I read yesterday's entry:

Sunday — 148 days

Dear Diary,
I have reason to believe that there is a SPY in the house. Somebody — some STINKY LITTLE BUSYBODY — has been reading my diary. Only a ROTTEN, SMELLY, HORRIBLE LITTLE SNOOP would read someone else's most PRIVATE SECRET THOUGHTS, and I think I know who it is! If you are reading this now, YOU NOSY PARKER, then I hope that you are feeling ashamed of yourself . . . because you should be! I hope your long nosy-parker nose falls off and your eyeballs pop out of your head. I hate you for this and I will never forgive you. Sally.

P.S. Dear Diary, I cannot tell you my secret until I catch the SPY and kill her!

I drop the diary as if it has burned my fingers! How dare Sally accuse me of reading her diary? I nearly grab a pen and write on the page some terrible things about her before I remember that then she would know for sure that I have been looking at it.

But she does know! Suddenly I feel terrible. I put my face in my hands. I can feel my cheeks burning. How did she find out? I am always so careful to leave everything just as I find it, and she is always out of the house when I read it.

Right then I do feel ashamed and like a sneaky nosy parker. How can I ever talk to Sally again or look her straight in the eye? She'll never forgive me. I would never forgive me if I were her.

Then I think, maybe she doesn't really know that I read her diary. Maybe she is only trying to trap me. I decide not to say anything at all, just to carry on as normal. And if Sally accuses me to my face I'll cry and call her a liar. So I put everything back where it was—and just in time, too, because I have hardly finished straightening out her duvet when I hear her key turning in the front door.

Chapter 3

Sally says nothing to me all that evening. Maybe she doesn't know it was me who read her precious diary after all.

Dad makes us pizza for dinner as usual. I used to love pizza, but now I am sick of the sight of them and Dad always leaves them in too long and they get all burnt and hard. "Sorry about that, kids," he mutters as he serves us a half pizza each. He doesn't seem to mind as he chews on his own piece of pizza as if he were chewing an old shoe.

Conor doesn't seem to mind either — he just eats away and talks to Dad about the soccer tournament and doesn't seem even to notice that Dad is barely answering him. "Liverpool are away to Man U on Wednesday, Dad," he says, his mouth half full.

"Is that so?" mumbles Dad as if he is living on another planet.

"Should be a close match. Man U will miss Rooney—he's pulled a hamstring."

"Is that so?" answers Dad, but I don't think he's even listening. Conor might as well be talking to himself.

Sally and I don't eat Dad's pizza if we can help it. Sally usually just walks over to the back door, opens it, and tosses her pizza out to our dog, Sparkler. After a bit I do too. Dad doesn't seem to care—but Sparkler is delighted. She never gets sick of pizza. When Mammy was alive, Sparkler used to charge around the house, jumping on everybody and licking them. Or she'd find her leash and pull it around in her mouth until somebody took her for a walk. Now she's never in the house and nobody bothers with her much, and she's gotten so fat from all the pizza that I don't think she could actually walk very far anymore.

After dinner Dad wanders off to look at some old photos, and that just makes him sadder. Conor takes his plate up to his room and starts playing his drums. He does that every evening now. He is the worst drummer in the world, and he is also the loudest. The noise he makes is so loud that I have to turn the TV volume up to its highest and Sally has to turn her CD player as high as it will go.

We live in a sad house but at least it is not quiet!

My friend Orla is very jealous of me because she has to be in bed by nine thirty every night and I can stay up as long as I like, but tonight I am tired and there is nothing on the TV so I go to bed at ten thirty. Orla is jealous too because I can just throw my clothes wherever I like and Aunt B. will pick them up in the morning. Aunt B. comes every day when we're in school and cleans the house spick-and-span, and every evening after school we mess it up again.

I used to find it hard to sleep with all the noise in our house. But you can get used to anything, and after a few words with Socky my eyes begin to close and my thumb slips into my mouth. "Good night, Socky," I tell my sock puppet, and he nods and says, "Good night, you." And then I slip him off my hand and tuck him under my pillow.

Before Mammy died I had gotten too old for Socky, but Mammy always used to look for him when she tucked me in. "Ah, poor Socky!" she'd say, and she'd pull him out, all dusty from under the bed, and then she'd put her hand into him and talk to him in her silly voice: "So, Socky, has Mimi got too big and grown-up for you, is that it? And I suppose she's too grown-up for a tickle from her old friend Socky too?" And then she'd tickle me to death with Socky on her hand. When she'd leave the room I'd throw him under the bed again. But since Mammy died I am not too old for Socky anymore.

The last thing I do before I drift off is to whisper "Good night" to the picture of Mammy on my nightstand, and I ask her to mend Daddy's broken heart. That makes me cry a little, but next thing I'm asleep.

Chapter 4

Tuesday — 150 days since Mammy died

Tuesday is Aunt M.'s day. Aunt M.'s full name is Marigold. Both my mammy's sisters are named after flowers — Aunt M. and Aunt L., whose full name is Aunt Lupin ("Aunt Loopy" my dad used to call her before Mammy died) — and my mammy was named Poppy. Daddy has only one sister, Aunt B., short for Betty — "Which is not a flower, thank you very much," she says!

Before I go to Aunt M.'s I have to drop in to Mrs. Lemon's shop for a Spiff bar and some free sweets. I love Mrs. Lemon.

Sally has detention today, so I am first to arrive at Aunt M.'s apartment, which suits me fine because

Sally keeps giving me these looks where she makes her eyes all narrow, and although she hasn't said anything I think she knows that I am the one who read her diary. So just at the moment I prefer to keep out of her way.

Aunt M.'s apartment is on the third floor, so I take the elevator. Her apartment is almost new, and even though Grandad says that you couldn't swing a cat in it, I think it is just perfect. Granny isn't too impressed with it either. She wonders where the children will play, but Aunt M. just says that she has no intention of having children for years and years, if ever, and Granny says, "We'll see about that."

"I'm not even married yet and you're going on about children already!" shouts Aunt M. She and Granny are always fighting.

Aunt M. will be married next September, to Nicholas—and he'll be dropping in later, says Aunt M. when she stops hugging me, so Conor will be pleased. Aunt M. always hugs me when I come on a Tuesday. If Sally is there with me, and she is in the mood, we have a group hug.

Aunt M. is very short—I'm nearly as tall as her—and she smells of those little blue flowers that I love, so I take a big sniff and say, "You smell lovely, Aunt M."

Aunt M. is an engineer, whatever that is, and Tuesday is her only half day, which is why she takes us after school on Tuesdays. Aunt M. is not one for baking, but she still has lots of goodies for us from the shop. So before *Southsiders* starts, Aunt M. and I have a good gossip and stuff our faces with sweets and bars and wash it all down with Coke, and then at three thirty we sit down on her white leather sofa and watch *Southsiders* together. Because Aunt M. misses every episode except Tuesday's I have to fill her in on what's been happening.

"Well, you'll never guess," I tell her. "Blackson—you know Blackson, the one with the ginger hair."

"The one who's going out with Ginger, the skinny girl with the black hair?"

"Yeah, well you'll never guess," I tell her. "Blackson walked into the pub, unexpected, and there was Ginger kissing guess who?"

"OH MY GOD!" screeches Aunt M., covering her mouth with her hand. "Who?"

"William!"

"No! Is he the one with the fair hair and the mustache who I fancy?"

"No, not him." Aunt M. is always getting the people in *Southsiders* all mixed up. "No, Gregory is the one you fancy—there's William!" I tell her, pointing at the screen, because William has just appeared . . . and he doesn't know it but Blackson is coming up behind him looking very mad indeed.

"OH, MY GOD! I CAN'T LOOK!" screams Aunt M., covering her eyes with a cushion as Blackson raises a big stick and is about to bash William on the head. . . . And then there's a commercial break.

Of course during the break Sally arrives. She stuffs a candy bar into her mouth and says, "I suppose you're watching that rubbish *Southsiders.*"

Then Aunt M. wants to show her her wedding dress before Nicholas arrives.

"I suppose it's white," Sally grunts, but Aunt M. just laughs.

So I am left watching the rest of the show on my own, and it's just not the same. I could kill Sally . . . if she doesn't kill me first for being a nosy-parker spy.

At last Aunt M. remembers me, but no sooner has she sat down again than Nicholas and Conor arrive at the same time, and suddenly Aunt M.'s cozy little apartment seems crowded with noisy people. Everybody has forgotten about *Southsiders,* and William will just have to bleed to death on his own because Nicholas has decided that I have watched enough TV.

"I wonder, will this round helmet fit on Mimi's

square head?" Nicholas shouts, and pushes his motorbike helmet onto my head back to front. He says I have a square head from watching too much TV but it's not true—I check my head regularly in the bathroom mirror and it is as round as it always was.

I can't see a thing with the helmet backward on my head, and then he starts to tickle me. Nicholas has the longest fingers that dig right into you and tickle you to death, and I'm nearly feeling sick with giggling when at last he stops because he has to talk seriously about motorbikes with Conor.

"Give me back my helmet, Squarehead," he says, and pulls the helmet off my head.

But before he goes he has to give his "fiancée" (that's what he calls Aunt M.) a big sloppery kiss, and Sally groans, "Oh, give me a bucket!" and Conor just goes red and looks down at his shoes until they're finished.

I wish every day was Tuesday. So does Conor because Nicholas takes him on a ride on the back of his motorbike. Sally loves Tuesdays too because she thinks Aunt M. is cool (I know that because I read it in her diary). So I am always sad when we have to go home to our sad house at six o'clock.

Today Dad is at least awake. He's just staring at the telly, although it is not even switched on. "Help yourself to pizza," he says, but even from the hall I can smell it burning.

Anyway, I'm still stuffed from Aunt M.'s and I still have my Spiff bar left, so I toss my pizza out to Sparkler, and so does Sally. Conor takes his black pizza up to his room and the drums start, and Sally's music starts blaring and I have to turn the TV up all the way to hear anything.

Chapter 5

Wednesday — 151 days since Mammy died

My teacher is named Ms. Addle. Orla says that is because she is always addled. Orla says *addled* means "scatterbrained" but I don't care because she is the nicest teacher in the school, probably in the world. But she *is* very addled, and now that she is pregnant she is more addled than ever. She is sitting in her chair with her legs stretched out and her hands under her big, round tummy when I walk into class. Most teachers don't like you to come in late every day, but Ms. Addle doesn't mind. In fact, she doesn't even seem to notice. So I come in late every day, sometimes very late.

I sit down beside Orla in the last row. Ms. Addle

is talking about her baby again, so Orla tells me a joke.

"This baby feels like it is going to pop out any day now, children—you know I haven't seen my feet for months!" Ms. Addle tells the class.

"This blond girl accidentally sets her house on fire," whispers Orla. Orla has lots of jokes, and lots of them are about stupid blond girls, which is a bit odd because Orla has long blond hair herself and she is the cleverest girl in the class.

"So take out your homework, everyone," says Ms. Addle.

Orla stops telling her joke for a minute while she takes out her homework. I wait because I have no homework to take out. "So anyway," she goes on, "the blond phones the fire brigade and tells them to come quick and put out the fire in her house. . . ."

I don't do my homework except on Wednesdays—Aunt B. makes me do it on that day, but otherwise I never do it. Ms. Addle doesn't mind. She is very understanding. She says she knows how hard it must be for me without my mammy. You see, she is the nicest teacher in the world. I love Ms. Addle.

"'How do we get there?' asks the fireman," continues Orla in a loud whisper. "'HELLOOOO,' says the blonde, 'IN THE BIG RED TRUCK, OF COURSE!'"

I wait for the next line. But that's all.

"Do you get it?" asks Orla, pushing her glasses up her nose.

"No," I tell her, scratching my head. I don't get lots of Orla's jokes, and she's about to explain it to me when the teacher asks her to read out her answer, so I'm saved. Because I never understand Orla's explanations either.

Recess is as horrible as ever. Sarah and her gang pick on me and Orla as usual. "Teacher's pet Crybaby didn't get her homework done again," Sarah says in her nasty squeaky voice, her face right up in mine. "Too sad, were we?"—and her two lapdogs (that's what Orla calls Sarah's two friends) laugh like crazy. "Maybe Specs will tell you a funny little joke to cheer you up," she jeers, punching Orla on the arm. Then they run off, laughing loudly in their ugly way.

I hate that girl. She wasn't always like that. When my mammy died I had lots of friends. Everyone would give me hugs and sweets in the yard and feel sad with me. But then Sarah started calling me Crybaby and hit the girls who came near me. So they didn't anymore—except for Orla, no matter how much she was teased. Orla says that she is a tough cookie and won't be intimibaited by a two-bit scumbag like Sarah

Sinclair. No, sireee! And the way she says that always makes me laugh.

"Let's make a voodoo doll of her and stick pins in it," says Orla. But I don't know what she is talking about and I don't really care. I just stare at the ground, and everyone in the school yard stares at me and Orla, but they keep away because they don't want Sarah to pick on them. Maybe she's right—maybe I am a Crybaby.

After school I go into Mrs. Lemon's shop to buy a candy bar with the rest of my lunch money, and Mrs. Lemon says, "Well, what can I do for you today, Miss Mimi?" I ask her for a Spiff bar, and after I have paid she takes some sweets out of the Pick 'n' Mix and puts them in my hand and closes my fist over them. Then she shows me her new CCTV camera, which she had to get installed because some children are not as honest as me and Sally and they steal stuff, and she hopes that the camera will help her catch them.

Then I have to go, because Wednesday is Aunt B.'s day and you don't keep Aunt B. waiting!

Chapter 6

Aunt B. runs a tight ship, Mammy always used to say. No messing, no dawdling, no wasting time. I never knew what she meant, but now that I go to Aunt B.'s every Wednesday half-day, I am beginning to understand.

When I arrive, my favorite cousin in the world, Emma, opens the door. "Well, hello, Dig!" she greets me, and we do our silly handshake and I say, "Well, hello, Dag!" and then it's straight into the kitchen chop-chop for lunch before homework.

We have to make our own lunch at Aunt B.'s house, but she supervises. Today we are having pancakes, and Aunt B. is giving orders. "Sally, sieve six ounces of white flour into the big white bowl. Chop-chop!"

(Sally has a half day on Wednesday too — and she always manages to get to Aunt B.'s before me so she can chat to cousin Emmett — and Conor will come along straight after school as well.)

"Emma and Mimi, beat up four eggs and don't get shell in the bowl. Chop-chop! Emmett, heat up the frying pan!"

Nobody argues with Aunt B., and soon we are all eating the most delicious pancakes — properly, with knives and forks. Aunt B. believes good table manners are very important. It's just as well she never eats at our house.

When we have finished, Emmett and Sally wash up and Emma and I dry the dishes.

"Come on, Sally! Chop-chop!" says Emma as she waits for Sally to finish washing the pan.

"Chop-chop yourself," says Sally, and splashes some soap in Emma's face.

Emma doesn't care — she just sticks out her tongue at Sally when Aunt B. is not looking. Aunt B. is not one for messing about.

Wednesday is the only day of the week when I do my homework, because Aunt B. makes sure I do. Nobody talks during homework. When Conor arrives, Aunt B. gives him three pancakes that she has kept for him and then he gets straight down to homework as well.

I know it sounds a bit strange, but I quite like it when the five of us sit around the table, all doing our work quietly. It feels like an office, and Aunt B. is the boss. Aunt B. never gets cross, yet we all do what she says without arguing.

Emma and I are always finished first because we are the youngest (Emma is six days older than me), so we can go and play. Nobody watches television before six o'clock in Aunt B.'s house, and if the weather is OK we have to play outside, but today it has begun to rain, so we play Dig and Dag in Emma's bedroom.

Dig and Dag are very old and they live in bed (just like the grandparents in *Charlie and the Chocolate Factory*). Dig, that's me, is the old man, and Dag, that's Emma, is the old woman. Dig lives at the top of the bed and Dag lives at the bottom. Today they are not feeling their best.

"You're looking a bit off-color today, lovey," says Dig.

"I'm not so good today, dear," answers Dag. "Me head is not so good."

"Aw, lovey dovey," says Dig, "are you feeling a bit soft in the head?"

"I am a bit soft in the head all right."

"You should put vinegar in your ears, lovey," suggests Dig. "I'm told that's great."

"I'd love a cup of tea, dear," says Dag.

"You drink too much tea, Dag. That's the reason why you have such a big yellow nose."

"I do not have a yellow nose, Dig!"

"You do so—it's big and yellow and snotty like a baboon's bottom!"

"Well it's better than having a big windy backside like you have, Dig," replies Dag angrily, "blowing out big smellies like the west wind all day!"

"How dare you say that I'm a stinker, you big hairy monkey!" shouts Dig—and then, quite by accident, I let out a big loud cracker-bum and Emma falls out of the bed laughing and we both have to run out of the room, holding our noses and giggling.

Sally and Conor and Emmett play on the PlayStation after their homework is done, but not very seriously because mostly they seem to be chatting and laughing.

At six o'clock Uncle Horace arrives home and his big loud voice booms throughout the house. Uncle Horace is a big hairy man, and wherever he is he seems to fill up the whole room. Aunt B. is always giving it to him, but he just laughs at her. He is the only one I know who is not a little bit afraid of Aunt B.

Uncle Horace always shakes your hand. His great big paw closes right over my hand and he squeezes.

"Ow!" I cry.

"Go easy, Horace," snaps Aunt B. "You're hurting the child!"

"Not at all," laughs Uncle Horace. "Am I hurting you, Mimi?"

"Just a little, Uncle Horace," I say, because I know he doesn't mean to. When he lets my hand go, my fingers are like squashed sausages. Uncle Horace is a doctor — I feel sorry for his patients.

We all have dinner at Aunt B.'s. Everybody sits around the table and eats their food with a knife and fork and nobody leaves the table until Aunt B. says so. All through the meal Uncle Horace talks about money, and you never know when he will throw a question at you so you have to stay awake.

"Conor, you are the great mathematician in the family, I believe, so answer this one if you can!" he booms at Conor. "Let's say Mimi has ninety-six cents in her pocket." And he winks at me.

"I don't have any money, Uncle Horace," I say.

"I know that, Mimi," he laughs. "Just bear with me! Now she has only one-cent, five-cent, and ten-cent coins, but she has the same number of each. The question is: how many coins has Mimi got in her pocket?"

"None!" I say, and everyone laughs at me.

But Conor is puzzling it out, his forehead all wrinkled up. I'm afraid I can't help him.

"Let the boy eat his dinner," says Aunt B.

Then Emmett says he has the answer, but Conor shouts, "Don't say it—I want to work it out myself!"

And he does, too. Conor is very clever.

"Bravo!" shouts Uncle Horace, and slaps the table.

After dinner Uncle Horace drives us home in his big Citroën car.

At home it is still bright and Dad is staring out of the front window. I stand with him, and he puts his hand on my shoulder. "Do you think she will try and pick it up?" he asks.

At first I don't know what he is talking about; then I see a lady walking toward our house and I understand. Before Mammy died, Dad stuck a euro coin onto the pavement with superglue to catch out Uncle Horace.

"Do you remember Mammy nearly splitting her sides when Uncle Horace tried to pick up the coin?" Dad asks sadly.

I remember very well. Uncle Horace's eyes lit up when he saw the coin and then he spent about five minutes trying to pick it up and getting all red in the face. In the end he looked up and saw us all in the front window laughing our heads off.

The coin is still stuck to the path, and it's still funny to see people who pass the house bending down to try and pick it up, but today the lady walks right past it without noticing.

"Ah, they were the good days," mutters Dad, and he wanders out of the darkening room, leaving me on my own.

Orla texts me a joke before I go to bed, which makes me feel less lonely even though I don't really get it:

How do u no that owls r cleverer than chickens? Ever heard of Kentucky Fried Owl?

Nite. C u 2moro. Luv O.

Chapter 7

Thursday — 152 days since Mammy died

This morning I didn't want to go to school. I just wanted to stay in bed and make up chats with Socky. And I wanted to read Sally's diary again when she had gone. Dad wouldn't have minded if I'd stayed at home—he probably wouldn't even have noticed. But Aunt B. would not have been pleased when she came by after ten to clean the house and wash our clothes. If I'd told her I felt sick, she'd probably just have given me one of her I-don't-believe-a-word-of-it looks and packed me off to school chop-chop no more nonsense young lady. So I dragged myself out of bed and off to school. I probably wouldn't have been so tired if Conor hadn't decided to bash away at his drums until two in the morning.

However, am I glad that I went to school today—it was the most exciting day for ages. We had all just sat down and taken out our homework (yes, even me—it was Thursday, after all), when Ms. Addle suddenly clutched her huge tummy and went, "OOOOOOOOO-OOOOWWWWWWWWWWWWWWWWWW!" And then she sat down very heavily with her legs sticking out like straws and breathing in and blowing out like a bag-pipe—her eyes all wide and her cheeks all blown up. And then, "OOOOOOOOOOOOOOOOWWWWWWWW-WWWWWWW!" again. And then she told her tummy in a panicky kind of voice, "You're not supposed to come for another three weeks!"

"Are you having the baby now, Ms. Addle?" said Dylan.

"I hope not!" said Ms. Addle, and then, "OOOOOO-OOOOOOOOWWWWWW!"

"She's having contraptions," whispered Orla. Orla's cat had kittens last week, so she's a bit of an expert on having babies.

Nobody knew what to do—everyone just sat and stared. Then Ms. Addle said, "Dylan, go and get Archibald, quick!"

Of course Dylan didn't know who Archibald was, so he didn't move—but I knew who Archibald was, because I had heard Ms. Addle call him that once. "She means Mr. Masters, Dylan," I said. And Dylan said "Oh" and hurried out of the room to get him.

"OOOOOOOOOOOOOOOOOOOOOOWWWWWW-WWWWW!" roared Ms. Addle. "They're getting closer!"

Mr. Masters is the principal of our school and even though they have different last names, he is Ms. Addle's husband, which is very strange because she's so nice and kind and, well . . . addled, and he is so horrible and efficient and everything goes right on time in his school.

But today Mr. Archibald Masters was completely addled too! He came running into the room with fat little Ms. Print, the secretary, puffing behind him. "Aggie, what's happening?" he shouted at Ms. Addle as he came tearing through the door. I don't think he noticed us at all. We were all out of our seats now and the classroom was in chaos.

"The baby is coming, that's what's happening!" Ms. Addle spoke quite sharply, but Mr. Masters didn't seem to notice.

"How far apart are the contractions? Are you doing the breathing? Somebody call a taxi! You will be all right, love. I've got everything under control!"

"For heaven's sake, calm down and go and get the car, Archie!" shouted Ms. Addle. But before he could say a word she let out another great roar:

"OOOOOOOOOOOOOOOOOOOOOOOOOOOOWWWW-WWWWWWWWW!"

"Oh, my God!" shouted Archie.

"You'd think it was Mr. Masters who was going to have the baby!" whispered Orla, and I nearly started giggling.

Then Ms. Print took over. "Mr. Masters, calm down—this isn't the first, nor will it be the last, baby to decide to come a little early. Now go and get the car and bring it around to the side door. And now, Aggie, hold my hand, and when the next pain comes, breathe through it nice and calm like they showed you in the prenatal classes."

Well, this was a whole new side of Ms. Print that we had never seen before; she should be running the school. Mr. Masters straightened his tie, took a deep breath, and then sprinted out of the room to get his car. Ms. Addle took Ms. Print's hand and started doing deep breaths with her, which seemed to help because Ms. Addle stopped screaming.

Then Ms. Print turned to us children who were crowding around in amazement. "Now, children," she said, smiling, "all of you go back to your seats and read your books; everything is just fine. Mr. Masters is going to drive Ms. Addle to the hospital so that she can have her baby, and I am going to go with them. Mr. Rogers will look after you."

Everybody did just as Ms. Print said, and Sarah the big bully was sent to get Mr. Rogers. Ms. Addle smiled weakly at us and said, "Isn't this exciting?" She was much calmer now, but I bet she was glad that Ms. Print was going to the hospital with her — especially when we heard Mr. Masters's car squealing to a stop outside our window.

In he charged like a mad bull, and he was about to grab Ms. Addle when Ms. Print held up her hand and said, "Just open the back door of the car and I'll help Aggie out."

We watched as Ms. Addle slowly slid into the car, helped by Ms. Print. Mr. Masters held the door and jiggled his keys, and Mr. Rogers said, "Give them a cheer" as the car pulled away.

"You go, girl!" shouted Orla out of the window, and everybody cheered. Ms. Addle waved bravely as they drove off.

So you see I was right to go to school today after all.

But it wasn't all good. Mrs. Lemon did not give me any free sweets today when I dropped in. She just took my money for the Spiff bar and looked sadly at me and said nothing.

Chapter 8

Sally didn't come straight home so I read her diary. I had to find out whether she knows it was me. But I'm still not sure if she is sure or if she is just pretending she knows so I will fall into her trap and give myself away. No fear of that—I was extra careful to put the diary back exactly as I found it and to straighten her bed so it was just as smooth as Aunt B. had left it. This is what she wrote yesterday:

151 days.

Hi spy, hoping to read something good today? Hoping to stick your nosy-parker nose into some juicy secret? Sorry to disappoint you, but I won't be telling any more secrets until I have hunted you down and dealt with you as you deserve! No mercy for sneaky spies.

I can tell you I didn't like the sound of that.

I wish that I had hair as black as Mimi's. Black is the only color I want in my life. I love going to Aunt B.'s and chatting with Emmett. Aunt B. is so cool—always stern, no nonsense. I'm going to be like Aunt B. when I grow up, and everyone will be scared of me. Nobody will dare to spy on my diary.

I'm so angry now, and I'm really afraid that I'll be caught if I don't stop but I just can't stop. Nobody would like me if they knew. I wish Dad cared. Why didn't Mammy take more care on the bike? I hate my life. Good-bye, spy.

When I had put away the diary super-carefully I brushed my hair in front of Sally's mirror. Sally loves my long, straight black hair. Black as black. But I hate it. I wish I had blond hair like Sally's (her hair is blond under the black dye). And I wish that I hadn't gotten slanty eyes — but Orla says she would love to have eyes like mine.

Wouldn't it be cool if people could swap body parts? I'll swap you my nose for your ears — or my sticky-out belly button for your sticky-in one?

I decided there and then never to read Sally's boring diary ever again. What's she afraid of, anyway? And why is she always angry? I hate black!

I really wanted to tell somebody about Ms. Addle and her contraptions, but Dad was just sitting looking blankly at the television. I bet if I switched it off he wouldn't even notice. So I rang Granny — and boy, was she interested!

She asked me heaps of questions and made me repeat the bit about Mr. Masters getting all panicky, and then she made me tell the whole story over again to Grandad. In the end I was about two hours on the phone but it was really good to talk.

"Did you tell all that to your daddy, Mimi?" asked Granny in the end. I told her no, that he wasn't in the mood, and she said to put him on the phone, so I handed the phone to Dad and told him Granny wanted to speak to him.

Dad sighed really loudly and took the phone. Even then I could still hear Granny giving it to Dad in a very loud, cross voice. Dad just kept saying, "Yes." "Yes." "I know." "I will." "I will."

When he put down the phone, he sighed again and pulled me over to him and I sat on his knee.

"So you had an exciting day in school today, did you? Well, I want to hear all about it."

When I had finished telling Dad the whole story, he laughed, and that was the first time I have heard him laugh since Mammy died. Then he gave me a big hug and told me to run along to bed.

Chapter 9

Sunday — 155 days since Mammy died

Weekends have become so long and so boring since Mammy died. We never do anything anymore. When Mammy was alive we always had family fun on the weekend. We used to go swimming on Saturdays — not anymore. If it was nice on Sundays we went for a hike, Daddy and Mammy and Conor and Sally and Sparkler and me. Actually I never really liked the hikes, but the funny thing is I really miss them now. All we ever do in our house now is watch television and fight and listen to very loud music while Conor goes crazy on the drums.

But this Sunday is going to be different.

Aunt L. and Uncle Boris and wee Billy have come all the way from Belfast to Granny's house for the weekend to celebrate wee Billy's first birthday, and all my aunts and their husbands and my cousins will be there for a big knees-up, says Granny (whatever a "knees-up" is).

We almost didn't go because Dad said he didn't feel ready for a party quite yet, but first Granny and then Aunt L. got on the phone to him and told him what for! "You owe it to those poor children to put a brave face on things and start living again," I heard Granny say. I heard her say that because I listened in very quietly on the upstairs phone. Do you know what? I think I would be a good spy.

So now we are all in the car and on our way. Dad is still not too happy about it — he keeps sighing — but Sally and I are delighted. Sally keeps saying she can't wait to see "wee Billy" in her best Belfast accent. Conor pretends he doesn't care, but I know he's hoping that Nicholas will take him on his motorbike if Granny doesn't have a holy fit about it. I'm holding the big fire engine that Sally and I bought this morning for wee Billy.

We are the last to arrive. Every inch of the kitchen table is covered with cakes.

"Your granny has been baking all week," Grandad whispers loudly to me, "and that's only about half of the cakes she has baked, but she's eaten all the rest herself. No wonder she's so fat!" And he winks at me.

"I heard that, old man!" calls Granny from the hall.

Uncle Boris grabs me from behind and swings me right up into the air. "How's my wee lass?" he roars. Granny says that Uncle Boris does not know how to talk—only how to shout.

In the living room, Aunt L. is having a very serious talk with Daddy. Sally is holding wee Billy, and he is trying to pull her nose off. Sally is different when she is with babies; she forgets to be cool and serious. I wish Sally was always like that, laughing and giggling.

Conor and Emmett are out looking at Nicholas's motorbike, and Aunt M. is talking to Aunt B. about her favorite subject—weddings! Uncle Horace and Uncle Boris are talking about money. I go and look for Emma—but she finds me first.

"Hi, Dig. Still having trouble with those windy bottoms, lovey?"

"No, dear. I'm much better now, thank you. Except for my big toe," I tell her.

"Oh dearie, dearie me, that sounds bad. You'd better show it to me."

So I sit on the floor and pull off my shoe and sock.

My big toe is shiny blue—I colored it with a fluorescent blue marker before I came. “It got stuck in the tap when I was having a bath. What will I do, Dag?”

“Do you always stick your big toe up the tap when you have a bath, Dig?” asks Emma.

“Of course.”

“So do I. But this looks bad, Dig. Will I chop it off, lovey?”

“If you must, dear. Will it hurt, Dag?” I ask as Emma pulls a big plastic ax from wee Billy’s toy bag.

“It will hurt a little. Be brave, Dig.” And she starts chopping and I start yelling. Wee Billy hears the racket and wiggles out of Sally’s arms and totters over to us. Then he falls on top of me and tries to eat my toe. Sally runs over and grabs him and she falls on top of Emma and me and soon we are all rolling on the floor, giggling and laughing, and wee Billy thinks it’s a great game.

When we stop all tired out from laughing and wrestling, I notice that all the adults have stopped talking and are watching us and smiling, and Aunt L. has her arm around Daddy’s shoulder and I don’t know if he is smiling or crying. I think that he is doing both.

Then Aunt B. claps her hands and tells everybody to come and eat, chop-chop.

* * *

When wee Billy had blown out his candle five or six times (Grandad kept on relighting it and all the children helped wee Billy with the blowing), and everybody had sung "Happy Birthday to You" about five times, and wee Billy had put both his hands in the icing and wiped it all over Sally's face, Aunt B. made her announcement. "I have got a morning-only job in Besco supermarket, in the meat department," she said.

"Chop-chop!" shouted Emmett, who had been finishing off everybody's wine when they weren't looking and whose eyes looked all glassy. If Aunt B. found out she would kill him.

Then Aunt B. looked at me, then at Sally, and then at Conor and said, "Which means I won't be able to come over to your house in the mornings anymore to put manners on the place."

"Chop-chop!" shouted Emmett again, and Aunt B. gave him one of her looks.

"A toast to Betty the butcher!" called out Uncle Boris, lifting his glass of wine, which distracted Aunt B. and saved Emmett.

"Chop-chop!" shouted everyone, and lifted whatever glass they were holding, and then wee Billy said his very first words: "Chop-chop!" And everybody clapped and laughed.

* * *

As we were driving home I asked Sally if she would wash our clothes now because she was the oldest girl, and she thumped me on the arm.

"Yeah, that's right, Mimi, Sally will have to wash our clothes now," said Conor from the front seat, just teasing.

"I hate you, Conor," snarled Sally. "I hate you both!"

"Take a joke, Sally!" Conor snapped back, but Sally would not take a joke. She just sat there with her arms folded and her lips thin and stared out of the window.

Nobody spoke after that. Dad just drove the car.

Chapter 10

Monday — 156 days since Mammy died

Monday is Granny's day. It is usually a good day, but this Monday was a bad day.

First Bad Thing: I woke up dead late and I couldn't find my shoes for ages — but they were behind the sofa where I kicked them off last night, so that was OK.

Second Bad Thing: There was no milk in the house and I had to eat my cornflakes with water on them. Ugh!

Third Bad Thing: The car ran out of gas on the way to school, and Sally and I had to walk the rest of the way. Sally was raging. "This is so embarrassing!" she shouted at Dad. "You don't care about us at all, do you?" And then she slammed the car door shut and stormed off without waiting for me.

"Sorry," muttered Dad, looking totally fed up.

Fourth Bad Thing: My new teacher is horrible. Her name is Ms. Hardy, and she is the total opposite of Ms. Addle. By the way, Ms. Addle had a baby boy, Roger, and she sent us all her love. Archibald (that's what everyone calls Mr. Masters now, behind his back) came in and told us. He was trying to be all strict and businesslike, but he couldn't help smiling when he told us that Ms. Addle had had a boy. "And she sends you all her—*cough, cough*—love. Ms. Hardy will be your teacher for the next three months and you are to be very good for her. Is that clear?"

"Yes, Mr. Masters," we all answered together.

Fifth Bad Thing: Ms. Hardy does not like pupils to be late, and I was very late.

"And your name is?" was the first thing she said to me when I burst into the room at five past ten.

"Mimi."

"Well, Mimi, you are over an hour late. I take it you have a good excuse," she said in her cold, hard voice.

So I told her about waking up late and losing my shoes and Dad running out of gas, and she just looked at me and said nothing. When I was finished she just wrote something in her notebook and told me to sit down.

Sixth Bad Thing: Sarah was her usual disgusting horrible self during recess. "So Crybaby overslept and lost her shoes and Daddy let the car run out of gas, did he? So what excuse is it going to be tomorrow, Crybaby? The bed exploded? An elephant sat on the car? Your thumb fell off from all the sucking? I don't think Ms. Hardy likes you very much, Crybaby," and she punched my arm and ran off cackling with her gang.

"Losers," said Orla, but I'm not so sure. Maybe it's me and Orla who are the losers.

Seventh Bad Thing: Mrs. Lemon gave me no free sweets again. Why is everyone being so horrible?

Eighth Bad Thing: There was a power outage when I was at Granny's house. It happened one minute after Granny had put the buns in the oven. So no cakes. Can you believe it? And that's not the worst part . . . no telly either. How will I find out now if Ginger will be found in time before the tide comes in and drowns her?

Actually it wasn't all bad, because Grandad sent me up to the attic to find a lampshade he had thrown up there about ten years ago. He gave me a flashlight and I had to climb the stepladder and pull myself up through the hole in the ceiling and then he shouted up to me to be careful and to step only on the wooden beams or else I'd fall through the roof.

Granny was chatting with Sally in the kitchen, so she didn't know what we were up to or she would have had a fit. Anyway, I found the lampshade — but much better I also found a box of toys that my aunts and my mammy used to play with when they were little girls.

It was mostly dolls.

"The ones with missing heads or arms or legs belonged to your mother," explained Grandad when I spilled them all out on the living-room floor. "She loved to play doctor, and that always involved amputating some poor doll's head or leg or whatever."

Another good thing in a day full of bad things was that Grandad forgot to give me my chess lesson.

Ninth Bad Thing: Grandad crashed the jalopy into the pillar when he was reversing out of the gate. I was sitting in the back with Granny and Sally; Conor was in the front.

"Oops," said Grandad.

"OOPS!" screamed Granny. "Is that all you can say? Oops! You could have killed us all!"

Grandad didn't answer that, and we three children stayed very quiet. Grandad and Granny got out to inspect the damage. “Not too bad,” said Grandad. “Just a broken taillight.”

But Granny was speechless with rage. All the way home Grandad drove even slower than usual. He stopped at all the red lights. The atmosphere in the car was awful—nobody said a word. How many bad things can happen in a day?

Chapter 11

Actually a lot of bad things can happen in one day—too many for one chapter!

Tenth Bad Thing: Dinner. I usually don't care whether the pizza is burnt or not because I don't usually eat it, but today I was so hungry because I'd had no sweets or cakes that I ate my dinner and it was like chewing a tire.

Sally was hungry too and she was still cross with Dad about this morning. "This is horrible," she told him. "Disgusting, gross, vile, poisonous, inedible gunk! Can't you cook your children anything else except pizza? And you can't even cook pizza properly! I hate you!" And she flung the rest of her pizza in the trash (which was a pity because Sparkler would have enjoyed it). Then she ran out of the kitchen and up to her room and slammed her door so hard that the pictures on the wall shook.

She cried for hours and hours. I had to turn the telly up to top volume so as not to hear her. I wish Mammy was here.

Dad was upset too. He just sat in his chair and said nothing, but his forehead was all wrinkled up and his eyes were black and his lips were very thin. And he kept sighing.

Conor just disappeared up to his room and started hammering away at his drums.

Eleventh Bad Thing: The house is very messy because Aunt B. didn't come to tidy up. The breakfast bowls and plates are still dirty, and there seem to be a lot of lost clothes and shoes on the floor. The curtains have not even been opened in most of the rooms. Our house is turning into a dump.

Twelfth Bad Thing: The doorbell rang. Mona and Brian were standing at the door when I opened it. They are our neighbors and they are very nice people, but as Granny would say they keep themselves to themselves so we don't see too much of them — except in the summertime when they are out in their garden having barbecues. They have a little baby called Barry.

"Hello, Mimi," said Mona. "Can I speak to your

father, please?" She was very red in the face. Mona is the kind of woman who blushes all the time.

I stood behind Daddy when he came to the door.

"Hello, Paul," said Brian (Paul is Daddy's name).

"Hello, Brian. Hello, Mona," said Dad. "What can I do for you?"

"Well," began Brian, "I don't know where to begin, but . . ."

"We know how difficult it must be for you since Poppy, you know, passed away, but . . ." And then Mona went even redder and just looked down at her shoes.

"It's just that . . ." began Brian.

"We can't sleep!" blurted out Mona.

"And Barry can't sleep either," said Brian, "and it has to stop!"

"What has to stop?" asked Dad, looking puzzled—but I knew what they were talking about.

"The racket!" said Mona. "The awful racket every evening: the telly at top volume and the music at top volume and worst of all the drums . . . on and on nearly all night, every night. Bang, bang, bang, bang, on and on!" Mona was really red in the face.

Brian just nodded and nodded and looked very serious.

"Oh," said Daddy. And then he just stood and listened, and sure enough the telly was roaring in the front room and Conor was going mad on the drums and Sally had decided to turn on her music—at top volume. The house sounded like a carnival.

Dad bent his head to one side like a bird listening for worms. "It *is* noisy, isn't it?" he said, as if he was only noticing the noise for the first time.

"Yes!" said Mona and Brian together.

Now it was Daddy's turn to go red in the face.

"I'm so sorry," he said. "What have I been thinking? The noise is terrible! Why didn't you mention it before? I'm so embarrassed. It will stop straightaway. Don't you worry! I'm really sorry."

"Thank you, thank you," muttered Mona and Brian together as they backed away from the door.

Turning on his heel, Dad marched into the living room and switched off the TV. Then he marched straight upstairs and straight into Sally's room and yanked out the plug of her speakers. Next stop was Conor's room; Conor's mouth fell open when Dad grabbed the drumsticks out of his hands and marched straight back down the stairs, his neck as red as a beet.

That's when I decided to go to bed. Twelve is enough bad things for one day. I stuck my thumb in my mouth and told my photo of Mammy that I wasn't talking to her because it was all her fault for getting run over on the bike and leaving us to cope all by ourselves.

Chapter 12

Tuesday — 157 days since Mammy died

When I woke up the sun was streaming in through the window, and it was just lovely to lie there in my cozy little bed knowing that it was Saturday and I didn't have to get up for school. Has that ever happened to you? Have you ever woken up on a Tuesday and thought that it was a Saturday and rolled over and fallen asleep in the sun for another hour?

Well that's what happened to me on Tuesday. And when I did finally wake up and realize — oh, my God! — that it really was Tuesday, not Saturday, and I was going to be dead late for school again, I got in an awful panic.

Where was my uniform sweater? All my clothes were in a heap all over the floor. I threw them here and there and I found my sweater in the end, only there was a big blob of tomato sauce from my pizza all down the front of it—but it would have to do. My tie (yes, we have to wear a tie in school—can you believe it, in this day and age?) was nowhere to be found, so I just said "Sod that" in a real Sally way. Sally and Conor had already gone to school without calling me, of course. They are the meanest, horriblest sister and brother in the whole wide world.

When I found Dad sitting looking out of the kitchen window at the weeds, he turned and looked at me in surprise. "I thought you had gone to school," he said.

"Well, you thought wrong," I nearly shouted at him. "Now drive me to school!"

Luckily there was enough gas in the car this time. Unluckily Ms. Hardy caught me trying to sneak into the classroom while she was turned to face the blackboard. I might just have gotten away with it except that Sarah called out, "Ms. Hardy, Mimi is late again."

Ms. Hardy turned around and looked at me and then at Sarah. "Do you enjoy tattling, Sarah?" she asked her, and Sarah didn't know what to say. Then she turned to me and said, "Go and sit down, Mimi. I'll talk to you at recess."

I didn't have long to wait. I was so late that it was nearly recess already. All the other children walked out, and Sarah whispered, "You're dead meat," to me as she passed. I didn't know if she meant that she was going to kill me or that Ms. Hardy was going to kill me. I think she probably meant they both were. I was all alone in the classroom with Ms. Hardy. It was then I thought that today would have been a very good day to stay at home sick in bed—pity I didn't think about that earlier.

"So, Mimi, tell me, why were you late again today?" she asked—in quite a kind voice, but with teachers you can never be sure. They can be kind one minute and nasty as a mad dog the next, so I was careful.

"I woke up and thought it was Saturday so I went to sleep again, but it was really only Tuesday and then I couldn't find my school sweater but it was under all the other clothes, but no way could I find my tie. And then I had to get Daddy to stop staring out of the window and drive me to school."

Ms. Addle would have understood, that's for sure, but Ms. Hardy just looked at the blob of tomato sauce on my sweater and then she stuck her finger into it and sniffed it. "Tomato sauce?" she asked, and then before I could answer she said I had big dark rings under my eyes and asked what time did I go to bed?

I told her that I always went to bed at twelve or eleven or one in the morning or whenever I was tired, but sometimes I would be too tired to go up the stairs so I would stay up watching telly for another hour or two until I had the energy to climb up to bed.

"Ummmmmm," she said, "and what does your father say about that?"

I should have told her that since Mammy was killed on her bike by the 82 bus 157 days ago my daddy didn't care about anything anymore. But for some reason I couldn't say it. I just stood there and looked at the floor and waited for Ms. Hardy to shout at me.

But all she said was, "OK, Mimi, I want you to write ten lines for me, saying, 'I must not be late for school,' and give them to me tomorrow. Out you go and play now. And try to be on time tomorrow, please."

Chapter 13

Well, ten lines wasn't so bad. Ms. Hardy might not be such a tough cookie after all. That's what Orla calls her—"a tough cookie." Orla told me one of her jokes in the school yard to cheer me up: "How can you tell if there is an elephant in the fridge?"

Of course I hadn't a clue.

"You'd see its footprints in the butter." I must have looked puzzled because Orla started to explain. "You'd hardly need to look for footprints to spot an elephant in a fridge, would you?" she asked—but just then Sarah and her lapdogs appeared, so I didn't answer Orla.

"So, Crybaby . . ." the big bully began, but at that moment the bell rang and Mr. Masters roared at us to line up quietly. Archibald was not in such good humor today. In fact he was looking quite tired, so everybody lined up quickly and quietly.

"Saved by the bell," whispered Orla.

After recess, Ms. Hardy gave me thirty lines for not doing my homework and told me to do both days' homework for tomorrow. "The homework you don't do won't go away, you know," she said. "It will just pile up." I really miss Ms. Addle.

After school me and Sally and Conor had to go to Granny's before we went to Aunt M.'s because she was going to take us to the dentist. I don't mind the dentist, because he always says I've teeth as sharp as a tiger's and I have never had to get a filling or a tooth pulled out.

A strange thing happened when I went into Mrs. Lemon's shop. She came around the counter and gave me a big hug and said she was sorry for tarring me with the same brush. I wish to goodness people would stop talking in riddles. I didn't know what she was saying, but the good thing is she pressed some sweets into my hand again so she mustn't be tarring me with the same brush anymore.

Sally was waiting for me outside, but she didn't go in. I didn't give her any sweets because she is going to the dentist, and I ate only four of them myself. We walked silently to Granny's house. Conor was already there — he had gotten out of school early to go to the dentist. He wasn't worried either; nor was Sally. We have great teeth in our family — that's what the dentist told Mammy the last time we went.

We drove in the jalopy — Grandad at the wheel, singing at the top of his voice a funny old song about living in a yellow submarine.

"Keep your eyes on the road," snapped Granny. But Grandad just winked at Conor and, turning around in his seat, looked in Granny's eyes and changed his song to "You Are My Sunshine."

"Keep your eyes on the road!" shouted me and Sally and Granny together, and Grandad turned his head forward again and nobody was killed.

"What a bunch of nervous ninnies we have in the back today!" he told Conor, and slapped him on the knee.

Conor laughed, but Granny said, "Keep your hands on the wheel, old man!"

I couldn't help thinking that today was a much better day than yesterday. That was before I saw the dentist.

"Right, Mimi, up on that seat and open wide and let's see how those tiger teeth are doing," said Dr. George, the dentist.

I love the dentist's chair. It's longer than I am and he puts it right back almost like a bed, and then he pumps the pedal and up the chair lifts. Then he shines the big round light in my face, and his lady assistant hands him the poky thing and he holds my mouth open and starts poking my teeth.

"Aha," he mumbled, and poked some more. Then "Aha," again — but he didn't seem too happy. "When did you last brush your teeth, young lady?" he said.

Well that was a hard question, and I had no idea of the answer, so I said I couldn't remember, only with his fingers in my mouth it came out like "Hicantrehember."

"Aha," he mumbled again, and then told me to rinse out.

I love that bit. The lady assistant gives me the glass with the pink water and I spit into the little basin that is attached to the chair. It really is a brilliant chair; you could nearly live in it if it had a TV attached and maybe a microwave oven.

Then came the part where Dr. George always says, "Hop down, young lady, and keep looking after those tiger teeth." Only today he didn't say that. He left me sitting there and went to fetch Granny and had a long conversation with her in the hall, in whispers, but I could hear most of it and I didn't like the sound of any of it.

"Five fillings . . . early signs of gum disease . . . teeth totally neglected . . ."

Sally and Conor didn't do so well either. We all needed a pile of fillings, and the lady assistant made appointments for us. Then Dr. George gave us a big lecture about dental hygiene, and brushing our teeth morning and evening, and cutting down on sweets and eating raw carrots and apples and vegetables and stuff like that, and Granny stood there and listened to everything with her lips zipped.

The drive back to Aunt M.'s was a very quiet journey. When we passed the supermarket Granny told Grandad to park the jalopy. Then she went in and bought three new toothbrushes and three tubes of toothpaste and dental floss and mouthwash and a box of red tablets called disclosing tablets. She said the first thing that we would be doing at Aunt M.'s apartment was brushing our teeth . . . properly!

Chapter 14

Aunt M. had her usual pile of bars and sweets and fizzy drinks spread out on the table. It was a mouth-watering spread. I reached out and took a Spiff bar.

"Well, that lot can go, for starters," said Granny to Aunt M., taking the bar out of my hand and dropping it in the trash can.

Aunt M.'s eyes narrowed—but before she could explode, Grandad jumped in, "Might be a good idea, Marigold. These guys have just got a pretty bad report from the dentist. No more junk food for a while."

I could see that Aunt M. wasn't too pleased that all her treats had to go back in the cupboard, and I wasn't too pleased either, but at least she didn't start arguing with Granny. When Aunt M. and Granny start screaming at each other all hell breaks loose.

Instead of getting mad, Aunt M. took me and Sally to her tiny bathroom and showed us how to use the disclosing tablets. "Suck 'em and see," she said, and we sucked a red tablet each. So did Aunt M.

Well, my teeth and Sally's went all red but Aunt M.'s stayed white and shiny.

"You look like vampires!" she laughed. "Maybe Mum is right and you need to start eating properly." Aunt M. calls Granny Mum because she is her mum. Then she explained that the disclosing tablet showed all the dirty bacteria and rotten gunk on our teeth, and she didn't have any because she flossed and brushed her teeth properly for at least three minutes twice a day *and* she used mouthwash, and we'd better start doing the same or we would have false teeth before we were twenty. So we had to brush our teeth the way she showed us, up and down and forward and back and in and out until all the red had gone, and we had to floss with the string stuff and rinse and gargle and use the mouthwash. The flossing really did make my gums bleed, but Aunt M. said they would harden up soon enough. Then Conor came in to have a laugh at us, but Sally grabbed him and Aunt M. tried to shove a disclosing tablet in his mouth and he pulled backward and fell out of the bathroom onto his bum. When he looked up, Granny was standing over him with her arms folded and she told him to get in there and brush those teeth or she would sit on him.

"And you wouldn't like that!" laughed Grandad, his head in the newspaper, so Conor had no choice but to take the disclosing tablet.

"Your teeth are a disgrace, Conor," Sally told him, so he punched her arm. But Aunt M. said, "Stop that, you two!" and ordered Sally out of the bathroom because she was finished. Conor wanted to know where Nicholas was, but Aunt M. just said she didn't know and she didn't care, which meant that they had had another fight, I suppose.

Granny raised her eyes to heaven, but Grandad started chuckling behind the newspaper. "What's the boy done to you now, Marigold?" he asked.

"You won't believe it, Dad, but do you know what he wants to do? He wants us to go on his dirty old motorbike from the church to the hotel after the wedding. Can you believe that?"

"It sounds cool," said Conor. "I'd love that!"

"Oh, I know you would, Conor," blustered Aunt M., "but you are not the one getting married! Think of how it would look—me in my white wedding dress on the back of a motorbike with a helmet on my head!

If he doesn't start having a bit of sense soon, he can marry somebody else!"

"Really!" said Granny. "That boy is so immature sometimes."

"How dare you say that about my Nicholas?" shouted Aunt M., turning on Granny.

Grandad jumped up and clapped his hands, then declared that it was time to go and headed straight for the door, just in time to stop another great fight between Granny and Aunt M.

On the way back to our house, Granny stopped off at the supermarket and bought a big bag of fresh fruit and vegetables for Dad to cook.

"I wonder what Dad will say about that?" Sally whispered to me in the back.

Chapter 15

That evening was not great.

Granny and Grandad had a long talk with Dad, and I wouldn't have needed to listen outside the living-room door to know what they were discussing.

Granny said something about her having lost a daughter, too, and us children having lost a mother, and that it was time for Dad to pull himself together and be a proper father again. Grandad didn't say a lot, and Dad didn't say much either, but Granny was in full flight.

She told him that our teeth were falling out of our heads, and pizza every night was not in any way a proper diet for growing children, and that we needed fruits and vegetables and meat and all sorts of stuff like that. She didn't stop there, either: she told him the house was a disgrace, that I was walking around in a sweater covered in ketchup, that Sally needed a strong hand or she would go completely off the rails, and that Conor was going more and more into himself . . . and were any of the children doing any schoolwork at all? And what was going to happen when Dad went back to work?

"Dad's getting an earful," whispered Sally, who was listening outside the door with me. Conor was back upstairs banging his drums; he must have found his drumsticks again. Then we had to scurry into the kitchen because Granny was finished and heading for the door.

"Bye, kids," she shouted as she and Grandad left.

Dad didn't come to the front door. He just sat in the living room for a few minutes with a very red face and a very cross mouth.

"Right!" he said all of a sudden, jumping up out of his armchair. He pushed right past me at the door and charged up the stairs two steps at a time. "There are going to be some changes around here!" he shouted as he burst into Conor's room. "Did I or did I not say no more drumming?" he roared, and grabbing the two drumsticks from a startled Conor, he broke them both across his knee and flung them into the corner.

Poor Conor was speechless.

Then without another word to him Daddy charged down the stairs again, shouting at me and Sally, "Up to your rooms, you two, and do your homework. And don't let me hear the telly or your music, Sally. Dinner will be in half an hour!"

And I thought yesterday was bad. I sat in my room for the whole half hour and cried. After a while Sally came in quietly and put her arm around my shoulders and told me not to worry, that Dad would get over it soon and calm down and everything would be back to normal again. But that only made me cry more because I didn't want things to go back to the way they were with Dad all sad about the place. I wanted things to go back to the way they were before Mammy got run over by the 82 bus, when our house was a nice place to live.

But just then my cell phone beeped and it was a text from Orla—one of her stupid jokes, of course—and Sally made me read it out to her: What is the best way to catch a rabbit? Hide behind a bush and make a sound like a carrot. Lol Orla X X X.

Even though it was a very silly joke I started

giggling and crying at the same time, and so did Sally, and soon we were rolling on the bed in fits — and I can't explain why we were laughing so much because we were both so sad.

"Dinner's ready. Get down here now," called Dad, and his voice still sounded as angry as before.

"Let's go and see what five-star meal our father has cooked up for our delight," said Sally.

The table was set and there was a lot of smoke in the kitchen and a bad smell of something burning. Sally made a face at me behind Dad's back, and I had to put my hand over my mouth to stop laughing.

The dinner was disgusting. I thought Sally might like it, because nearly everything was black. Dad was obviously not the best cook in the world. There was a pile of soggy green stuff on each plate that was supposed to be peas, beside this hard black thing that curled up at the edges, which apparently was a pork chop. The potatoes — well, at least you could recognize them.

"Nobody leaves the table until every bit of that dinner is eaten," said Dad.

"You can't be serious. A dog wouldn't eat this!" said Sally, and pushed her plate into the middle of the table.

"You will do as you are told, miss," snapped back Dad. "There are going to be some changes around here, young lady."

It was as if the words that Granny had said to him had lit a fuse in Dad, and all his hanging around with a sad face was blown away and replaced by this really cross Dad, and I didn't like it one bit. Sometimes I just wish Granny would mind her own business.

Well, Conor ate the meal because he has a stomach like a trash bin, but he did not say a word to anyone and his eyes looked red and puffy. When he was finished he went straight back to his room and banged his door shut so hard that the plates on the table jumped.

Eventually I managed to finish my dinner, even though I felt like throwing up a few times. The meat had to be chewed about five hundred times before it would go down, and I found it helped if I closed my eyes when eating the peas. The potatoes were OK . . . ish.

Sally ate nothing. She just sat there with her mouth shut while her dinner got colder and colder and Dad got madder and madder. He ordered me to go to my room and get ready for bed and said he would be up later to see me brush my teeth. It was only seven o'clock, but going to bed sounded like a good idea.

In twenty minutes Dad came up to make sure I brushed my teeth properly. Sally was still at the table,

I supposed, because she hadn't appeared. Dad stood with his arms folded and his face very red while I brushed my teeth for three minutes. I don't think he heard the back door opening, but I did and it wasn't hard to guess what Sally was up to. I had had enough upset for one day, so I hopped into my bed and closed the door after Dad had given me a quick kiss and a stern "Good night." Even with the door closed I could hear Dad roaring at Sally for giving her perfectly good meal to Sparkler. It was the end of a lousy day, so I just pulled my pillow tight over my head to block out all the shouting, put my thumb in my mouth, and went to sleep without even saying good night to Mammy or Socky.

Chapter 16

Wednesday — 158 days since Mammy died

It was probably because I went to bed so early, or else it was the bright sun shining in my window, but whatever the reason I woke up bright and early. I knelt on my bed and pulled the curtains back and looked out into the back garden. We have a big back garden; the grass is very long, but even so it would have looked lovely in the sunshine if Sparkler hadn't been squatting in the middle of it doing her morning poop. The garden must be full of dog poop by now because nobody cleans it up.

Mammy was an "avid" gardener, which I think means that she was very good at it. She certainly spent a lot of her time gardening, and our garden was full of flowers. But she always left room for us to play, so there was plenty of grass and a swing and a big slide and a real tree house with a little wooden ladder up to it. Sally and I used to spend a lot of time in the tree house. We always had a bucket of water up there to throw down onto Conor and his friends when they decided to attack us. Nobody plays in the garden now — except Sparkler, who has turned it into a big toilet.

I was just thinking about all this when Dad burst in, which was a big surprise because he hardly ever comes into my room now. The other big surprise was that he wasn't tired and sad. "You're up early," he said cheerfully. "Now get dressed quickly, have your breakfast, and brush your teeth. And while you're doing all that I'm going to wash this lot, and then I'll take you to school." And with that he scooped a load of my clothes up off the floor and headed downstairs to throw them in the washing machine.

It was only when I was half dressed that I realized he had taken all my uniform except the tie. "Dad!" I yelled. "My uniform!"— but it was too late. It was already sloshing around in the washing machine. I wasn't too pleased.

"Oh, it's not the end of the world, Mimi. Put on something else and stop making a fuss!"

He was cross again, but it wasn't my fault. Sally wouldn't get out of bed and Conor had spilled milk all over the kitchen floor—by accident on purpose, I think. Dad was doing his best to do everything, but his mood was not getting any better.

"Brush your teeth, Mimi, *now,*" he barked at me, which was just so unfair because I was the only one doing what she was told. "One, two, three . . ." He was counting now at the top of his voice, and if Sally wasn't up by the time he got to ten he was grounding her for a week.

Sally got up exactly on ten and gave poor Dad one of her I-so-hate-you looks. By the time she was dressed it was nearly time to go.

"Eat your breakfast quickly. And brush your teeth," ordered Dad.

"I don't eat breakfast, which is something you would know if you showed any interest in us at all," Sally told him.

Conor and me were standing at the door, but Dad wouldn't go until Sally ate some breakfast.

Sally hates being late for school, so she shoveled down about three spoonfuls of cereal and looked as if she was going to throw up. "Satisfied?" she screamed at Dad, and grabbed her schoolbag. Black mascara was running down her nose where she hadn't had time to put it on right — or maybe she was crying.

"No," said Dad. "Go and brush your teeth . . . for three minutes."

"I hate you!" she screamed, and raced up to the bathroom. Dad timed her to make sure that she did the full three minutes. She nearly broke the car door, she slammed it so hard.

"Thanks, Sally," said Conor. "Now we're all going to be late!"

"Shut up, Conor!" she yelled, and started punching him. Luckily I was in the front.

"Stop it, you two, this minute!" roared Dad, and I wondered if things could get any worse.

Chapter 17

Yes, things could get worse. The whole class was working really quietly when I came in — dead late, of course, thanks to Sally. Twenty-seven heads turned to look at me, and I felt my face go red like a beet, although it didn't look a beet. Because I have brownish skin nobody can see when I blush, but I was blushing inside.

Ms. Hardy looked at her watch. "You are very late, Mimi," she said.

"I . . . I . . . I know," I faltered, and I could hear some children giggling.

"Quiet!" said Ms. Hardy. "Go and sit down, Mimi, and take out your homework. By the way, where is your uniform?"

“In the wash, Miss,” I whispered. “Daddy threw it all in the washing machine this morning before I could stop him.”

Again I heard children giggle.

“Just bring me up your homework, Mimi,” said Ms. Hardy, kindly enough — but how I wished that Ms. Addle was back teaching us again.

Of course I had no homework to show Ms. Hardy, so I just looked down at my desk. I didn’t feel so well and I had to swallow hard not to cry.

“Your lines?” asked Ms. Hardy — and that was too much. I started blubbering like a baby. I tried to wipe away my tears with the back of my hand, which only spread snot all over my face. Orla put her arm around my shoulders.

“Mimi’s mother was run over by a bus so she doesn’t do any homework, Miss, except on Wednesdays,” called out Sarah.

“Did I ask you, Sarah?” snapped Ms. Hardy, and glared at her.

“No, Miss,” muttered Sarah, and her face went bright red.

Then Ms. Hardy crouched down in front of my desk and talked quietly to me. I sniffed and sobbed but her voice, though soft, was firm. Ms. Addle would have hugged me and said never mind. “Mimi, I’m very sorry about your mother," Ms. Hardy said, "but that is not a reason to neglect your work. I expect you to do your homework every night and to come to school on time, in your full uniform, every morning. Pass in the missing homework and the lines tomorrow, please. Now, what is your home phone number?"

"Twoeightthreesevensixfournine," I called out in a rush.

"A little slower, Mimi," said Ms. Hardy, smiling.

"Two"—*sniff*—"eight"—*sniff*—"threeseven"—*sniff, sniff*—"sixfournine"—big *sniff*.

"Thank you," said Ms. Hardy when she had written down the number. "I think I'll have a little chat with your dad. Nothing for you to worry about."

"'I think I'll have a little chat with your dad. Nothing for you to worry about,'" sneered Sarah in the school yard, and pushed me over. "You're a pathetic loser and a Crybaby," she jeered, and her gang laughed like drains before they all walked off.

"Rotten lousy scumbags," whispered Orla as she helped me to my feet. "Did you hear what the policeman said to his tummy? 'You're under avest.'"

And even though I was feeling very sad I just had to laugh, because I got that joke and it was really a silly one.

Chapter 18

That afternoon I went straight to Aunt B.'s house. I didn't stop at Mrs. Lemon's shop because I was afraid if I got delayed Sarah would be waiting to kill me outside.

Emma answered the door. "Good day, Dig," she greeted me, and then gave me one of her celebrity hugs. Emma and I are going to be celebrities when we grow up, so we have to practice our hugs. "How are you, darling?" she asked in a hoity-toity voice.

"I am absolutely shattered, my dear Dag," I replied. "I have spent the whole day shopping. My poor legs are worn down to stumps, and my head is splitting!"

"What you need is an Indian head massage, my dear Dig," Emma said. "And I am just the one to give it to you." And then before I even had a chance to put down my bag, Emma shoved her fingers into my hair and started ruffling it all up.

"Stop," said Aunt B., appearing in the hall. "Now, chop-chop, girls, we have lunch to make."

Lunch was a chicken stir-fry that Aunt B. had prepared that very day at the butcher's. She just loved her new job, and she told us all about how you made sausages and black pudding out of dried pig's blood. Emma made a face at me when Aunt B. went to the door to let Sally in, but the chicken stir-fry, which I was given the job of stirring, certainly smelled yummy.

Emmett was with Sally and they had to set the table. Aunt B. put some stir-fry away for Conor. It was the nicest lunch I have had in ages—and to think that I made most of it myself. I might be a chef when I grow up—a celebrity chef.

We all washed the dishes together while Conor ate his lunch. He had a big bag of soccer gear with him.

"What's in the big bag?" Aunt B. asked him.

"All the dirty jerseys of the soccer team," he told her. "It's my turn to wash them."

Then we sat down to start our homework, which was a good thing because I had lots to do, and lines as well, for Ms. Hardy, but I had hardly gotten started when there was a ring at the door.

It was Dad! He didn't look too happy—but then again, he never did look too happy these days. "OK, you three," he ordered, "let's go."

"What?" said Sally. "It's much too early. We never go home at this time!"

"Well, we do today, Sally. Say good-bye to your cousins and say thank you to your Aunt B. and get in the car."

"What's the rush, Paul?" Aunt B. asked Dad. "Horace can drop the children home later."

"Thank you, but he will not, Betty," Dad told her. "Those children are coming home right now. Mimi's teacher rang me to come in to talk to her, and after I had seen her I paid a visit to Sally's and Conor's teachers as well, and I was horrified by what I was told . . . by all of them." He sounded very annoyed.

Conor put his head in his hands and groaned. Sally closed her eyes tightly and pursed her lips, and I went red under my skin.

"OK, kids," said Aunt B. in a surprisingly soft voice, "pack up your stuff and we'll see you again next week. OK now, chop-chop." And she helped me put my books into my bag and gave my shoulder a secret little squeeze.

I really would have liked to stay at Aunt B.'s house, but Dad was standing there with a face like thunder, jiggling the car keys.

Chapter 19

It was a quiet drive home. The situation did not look too good. Sally had her arms folded across her chest and just stared out of the side window with her lips thin and her eyes black. Conor looked fed up and kept turning his eyes to heaven every time Dad muttered something.

Nobody asked Dad what the teachers had actually said. I didn't like to think what Ms. Hardy might have said about me, but obviously I wasn't the only one in the family who had been doing badly in school.

As soon as we were through the front door Dad ordered us upstairs to do our homework and do it properly and not to reappear until we had it done, and to show him our homework when we had finished it so he could check it — and if he was not satisfied we would be going straight up to do it again.

"Yes, sir," muttered Sally, but I don't think Dad heard her. Which was just as well because he was in a bad mood.

I closed my door, threw my bag in the corner and myself on the bed, and pulled Socky onto my hand. "Hi, Socky," I whispered.

"Hi, Mimi," whispered Socky, his mouth opening in perfect time with the words. I might be a puppeteer when I grow up (when I'm not being a celebrity), but I still have to get the hang of ventril . . . ventrilo-something-or-other. That's when you talk without moving your lips. Your voice has to come out of your belly button, I think. It is very hard to do but you can do anything if you set your mind to it, I reckon. Anyway, that's what Mammy says — I mean, what she used to say.

I could hear Conor opening his door and going downstairs.

"Is he dinished alldeddy?" said Socky, and I swear my lips didn't move.

"Are you finished already?" I could hear Dad saying in an astonished voice.

"No," snapped Conor. "I just have to put all the soccer jerseys in the wash. It's my turn to wash them."

"Conor does not know how to kut on the hoshing hachine," said Socky. He sounded really quite convincing.

"Leave it," said Dad roughly. "I'll do it for you. You don't know the first thing about putting on a wash. Now get back upstairs." I could hear Conor tramping back up the stairs, and then Dad calling out, "Sally! Mimi! If either of you has any washing, throw it down now. I'm putting on a wash!"

I threw down my fluorescent red T-shirt and Sally flung a load of black clothes.

"You're welcome!" said Dad sarcastically as he picked them up off the hall floor.

"Thanks, Dad," I said, but Sally just flounced back into her room, slamming her door after her. She was in one of her moods.

I went back into my room too and sat down to do my homework. I didn't want to do it, but I decided I'd better or Dad might just kill me, so I threw Socky on the bed and opened up my math book.

Would you believe it? Fractions for homework. Fractions were invented by some evil madman who got his kicks out of making schoolchildren miserable.

"If there were twenty-five sweets in a bag and Anne ate three-fifths of them, how many sweets were left?"

I mean, who cares? Why didn't she just eat all

the sweets like a normal child? Then the problem would have been easy. She was probably one of those horrible girls who always saves some sweets for later so that they can suck them slowly in front of you when you've finished all your own, and you just feel like smacking them.

Anyway, there was no point in getting all worked up over some greedy little girl, so I just got on with the problem. Three-fifths of twenty-five—I mean, how hard can that be? Too hard for me! So I texted Orla.

Divide by the bottom and multiply by the top and subtract your answer from 25. Easy-peasy-lemon-squeezy. Luv u Orla.

That didn't sound too hard. So I had to divide twenty-five by five, which was the bottom of the fraction. If I'd had the sweets it would have been easier—because dividing is pretty tricky when you haven't done it for as long as I hadn't. So I started doing it on my fingers, but that didn't work so well because I don't have twenty-five fingers.

Then Dad called us down for dinner, which was a relief because I was starving—but it did make me lose count. At this rate I was never going to get my homework done.

Chapter 20

Dinner was a sad, quiet affair. Dad had made some sort of pig swill that was meant to be a stew, and you would have had to be starving to eat it. Or afraid that your father was going to kill you if you didn't. I was both. So I managed to get it down. Conor, of course, shoveled it in. I seriously think that he has no taste buds at all. Sally pushed her stew around the plate and ate the odd forkful. The fight seemed a bit knocked out of her — or else she just wanted to get away as quick as she could.

"So how's the homework going?" Dad asked no one in particular. So no one in particular answered. Dad seemed to be enjoying his dinner — he was already taking seconds. You can see clearly where Conor gets his sense of taste. "Conor? Any problems with your homework?" he asked the top of Conor's head. (When Conor eats, his nose nearly touches the plate.)

"No," said Conor.

"OK. How about you, Sally?"

Sally grunted something that nobody caught and Dad didn't ask her again.

"Do *you* need any help with your homework, Mimi?" Dad turned to me. He was trying to be helpful, and Conor and Sally were being so rude to him. I felt sorry for Dad, so I said that I *did* need help with math . . . which was true, actually.

So after dinner when the others had gone back to their rooms to finish their homework or whatever they were doing, I brought down my math book and sat down with Dad at the kitchen table. Mammy used to help me every day with my homework, and although we'd sometimes end up shouting at each other, I'd have done anything to have her back for one minute, even of shouting.

I was thinking about this while Dad read out the question. "Three-fifths of twenty-five. Right. First things first. Do you know what a fifth is?" he asked me.

"Not really," I had to admit.

"That's no problem," said Dad. "It's easily explained. Imagine a pizza."

"I'd prefer not to," I said with a little smile. The pizza that jumped into my mind was as black as an old tire . . . and it suddenly reminded me of Sparkler. "Hey, Dad—did anyone feed Sparkler?"

"Don't worry about Sparkler; I'll give her the left-overs of the stew later on. Now imagine the pizza is cut into five slices. Can you picture that?"

Poor old Sparkler was what I was thinking about, having to finish off that stew—but I didn't say it.

"Now picture this. There are twenty-five olives on the pizza. How many olives on each slice?"

At this stage, I was seriously sorry that I had asked for Dad's help at all. "I don't like olives," I said.

"Well, bits of pineapple, then. It doesn't really matter if it's olives or pineapples or lumps of rock!" said Dad, and his voice was getting a bit louder. So I was glad when at that very moment the doorbell rang.

Chapter 21

It was Mrs. Lemon from the shop. I don't think she had ever been to our house before. Well, maybe when Mammy died. Lots of people came then "to pay their respects," but otherwise for Mrs. Lemon this was a first.

"Hello, Mrs. Lemon," I said, opening the door wide.

"Hello, Mimi," said Mrs. Lemon in a quiet voice. "Can I speak to your father, please?"

I didn't have to call Dad because he was right behind me. I wasn't sure if he even knew Mrs. Lemon.

"What can I do for you, Mrs. . . . ?" he asked.

"Mrs. Lemon. From the shop," she explained. "Could I have a private word with you please, Mr.

Roche?" She nodded her head toward me in that way that adults have of saying, "Not in front of the kids, please."

So Dad told me to run along and finish my homework while he showed Mrs. Lemon into the sitting room — but I stayed behind the door and put my ear quietly up against it. I could hear almost every word.

Mrs. Lemon sounded very embarrassed. She kept apologizing and, at first, I didn't know what she was talking about. I was sure that Dad didn't have a clue either. It was worse than pizzas and olives.

"I'm really sorry to disturb you like this, Mr. Roche," she started, "because I know you must have enough on your plate since your wife died, and it can't be easy with three children . . . and they must be very upset . . . so I suppose you can't blame Sally for . . ." and she trailed off.

"You can't blame Sally for what?" said Dad.

"Mr. Roche, I can assure you that I haven't gone to the police about this, and I'm just so sorry to trouble you with —"

"The police?" repeated Dad, sounding a bit upset now.

The police? What had Sally done?

"You see, when I got the CCTV camera installed I didn't think anything of it. I didn't even know how to work it properly, to be honest with you, but stuff kept disappearing off the shelves."

"What stuff?" asked Dad.

Yeah, what stuff? I wanted to know.

"Well, stationery, mostly. Pens and markers and folders and such."

"I know what stationery is," said Dad, a bit rudely.

A bad thought was growing in my mind. I had to cover my mouth with my hand.

"Are you accusing my Sally of shoplifting, Mrs. Lemon?" said Dad very loudly and angrily. I wondered if Sally could hear him from her bedroom. "Because if you are, you are very much mistaken! I will have you know that my daughter Sally would never, *never* steal from anybody!"

I wished I felt as sure about that as Dad seemed to.

"Of course not. Of course not," wailed Mrs. Lemon, and she really was wailing now. "It's just that she is on the films. . . . Here, see for yourself. I'm really sorry."

It went quiet then. I could hear Dad pushing a DVD into the machine and the whirring sound it made. Oh, why was this stupid door not made of glass!

Then I heard Dad saying quietly, in a broken kind of voice, "Oh, no. Oh, no."

So I supposed Sally had been caught on camera after all.

"It's all right, Mr. Roche. It really is." I could hear Mrs. Lemon trying to console Dad. "I shouldn't have come. It's nothing really. She probably just misses her mother."

Then there was a sudden rushing sound and the door flew open. I nearly fell into the room—but Dad just rushed past me as if I wasn't there. "SALLY!" he yelled. "GET DOWN HERE AT ONCE!"

Chapter 22

At first Sally denied everything. She cried and wailed and said that it was all a big mistake and she even accused Mrs. Lemon of making it all up.

"So now you're lying on top of stealing," said Dad in a hard voice.

"Don't you trust me *at all*?" she shouted at Dad, who was standing there with his arms folded and his face like thunder.

Nobody seemed to notice me now, so I just sat quietly and watched. Even Conor had appeared. He was standing in the doorway. He said nothing but he was listening very intently.

Then Dad pressed PLAY on the remote, and the image of Sally came up on the screen. She looked all around, checking whether anyone else was there. There was nobody else near her, and in the background you could see Mrs. Lemon with her back turned. Then Sally grabbed a packet of markers and slipped them into her schoolbag. She was very quick, just like a real thief. It was a clear image and there was no mistaking her. Then she walked up to the counter and said, "Hello, Mrs. Lemon," as if butter wouldn't melt in her mouth. And then the picture showed Mrs. Lemon smiling at Sally and pressing some free sweets into her hand. That made me feel quite mad at Sally—but I felt sorry for her at the same time, because she was just standing there saying nothing now, tears running down her face, and she kept wringing her hands.

"I'm sorry, Sally," said Mrs. Lemon quietly. She was sitting in the middle of the sofa looking like a little mouse.

"It's not you who should be sorry, Mrs. Lemon," said Dad. "Sally, what got into you? Bringing shame on yourself and on this family. If your mother were alive today, she—"

But he didn't get to finish. Suddenly Sally looked up straight into Dad's eyes and screamed, "But she isn't, is she?" Then she ran out of the room and up the stairs and slammed the door of her room so hard that the house shook. Then she must have thrown herself onto her bed, because the light in the ceiling moved.

Everyone was quiet then, except for Mrs. Lemon, who was whimpering and sniffing into her handkerchief. "I shouldn't have said anything. I shouldn't have come."

Dad helped her to her feet and led her gently to the door. "Mrs. Lemon, I'm deeply sorry that this has happened, and I assure you that every item stolen from your shop will be paid for," he said in a very serious voice. "I do appreciate your not informing the police. I will be having a very serious word with Sally, and she will be appropriately reprimanded. I am deeply embarrassed and ashamed that my daughter should have caused you such upset."

Dad didn't come back into the sitting room when Mrs. Lemon left. He headed straight upstairs to Sally's room.

"Do you think Dad is going to kill her?" I asked Conor.

"Well she deserves it," said Conor. "But I think she's locked her door."

Sure enough, Dad was yelling through Sally's door,

ordering her to open it, but she wouldn't. Which I thought was a good idea under the circumstances.

Then my phone beeped. It was a text from Orla. Who steals soap from the bath? Robber ducks! Lol Orla X X.

I read it to Conor and we both started giggling, which was a bit strange when you think that our whole family was falling apart.

We both stopped pretty quick when we heard Dad coming back down the stairs. He was still shouting. "All right, have it your own way, Sally, but this isn't just going to go away, you know. There has never been a thief in this family before and, by God, there won't be one now. Lie on your bed and feel as sorry for yourself as you like, but you and I will talk about this tomorrow!"

Chapter 23

Thursday—150-something days since Mammy died

Can you believe it? I've lost count of the number of days it is since Mammy died. I'll have to check Sally's diary, which won't be too hard now that she's gone. It's the first day that Sally's been gone. The last time I heard her she was sobbing away on her bed. I thought she'd never stop. I tried to shut her out by putting my hands over my ears, but that didn't work. The walls in our house must be very thin, you can hear so much—which I don't usually mind, especially when people are on the phone and I can listen in. But last night I hated it. It was like the days after Mammy was killed, except that I was crying then as well and my pillow used to get all wet and horrible. I bet Sally's pillow was soaking last night. And she kept doing these gulps. I felt like going into her room and giving her a hug, but I knew that Dad would kill me if I got out of bed, and her door was locked, anyway.

I must have gone to sleep in the end because I didn't hear her leave. Nobody did. We didn't even know until it was time for school. Dad roared up at her a few times while Conor and I stood waiting in the hall, but there was no answer. Then he shouted that he had had quite enough of this carry-on and she'd better come out at once or he'd break down the door. I'd like to have seen that! Dad charging like a bull at Sally's door and flattening it just like the Incredible Hulk. But he didn't have to in the end because her door wasn't locked anymore, so he just turned the handle and walked in—and there was nobody there. Sally had gone.

Dad just stood there for a moment looking very cross, but then he went pale. He opened the wardrobe and looked inside, and then he bent down and looked under the bed. Of course, she wasn't there. Her bed was made (very unusual that), and Sally was gone.

"Where's Sally?" Dad turned to me.

"I don't know," I answered as fast as I could, but he didn't wait.

He pushed past me and raced down the stairs and out into the front garden and out into the middle of the road. Then he started looking up and down frantically. "Conor!" he shouted. "Do you know where she is?"

"No," said Conor.

Then Dad walked very quickly back into the house. "Stay calm, children," he said to Conor and me—but we *were* calm, at least compared with him. Then he was on the phone to Aunt B. and he wasn't calm at all. "Betty, she's gone!" he told her, and his voice was all shaky. Aunt B. must have asked who, because he said, "Sally, of course." Then he put down the phone and said that Aunt Betty was coming over and we weren't to panic, and that there was probably a perfectly reasonable explanation for Sally not being in her room, and had either of us heard anything at all last night, and what were the names of all her friends, and that it was probably too soon to ring the police. And while Dad was saying all that without even stopping to take a breath, he was wringing his hands together as though he was trying to get them clean.

I couldn't help it—I started to cry, because first Mammy was gone and now Sally was gone, and even though I knew it wasn't really the same thing I kept thinking, what if she doesn't come back *ever*?

Conor had his mobile phone out and he was trying to ring her. It was probably the first time he had ever tried to ring Sally. It was a surprise to me that he even had her number. He held the phone to his ear for a long time, but there was no answer.

"Try again," said Dad.

So Conor did, but this time the phone did not even ring. It went straight to voice mail.

Dad grabbed the phone off Conor. "Sally," he shouted, "pick up the phone at once. You have us worried sick. Where are you?"

But Sally did not pick up. Instead her phone went dead.

Dad slumped into a chair. He looked very old and worn-out all of a sudden. Conor put his hand on his shoulder, and I put my arms around his neck.

"It's going to be all right, Mimi," Dad said. "Sally will show up soon enough, you'll see." But his voice sounded flat and defeated, and I just knew he thought that she was gone forever, just like Mammy.

Then Aunt B. arrived in her car, and she must have rung Aunt M. because she was in her car right behind. Aunt B. stepped out from behind the wheel and walked quickly up the path, Aunt M. trotting along after her. "Paul, put on the kettle," she ordered Dad, "and you two go with Marigold. She'll take you to school. And Mimi . . ."

"Yes, Aunt B.?"

"Stop sniffling. Sally is going to be perfectly all right."

Chapter 24

On the way to school, Aunt M. told us to write down the names — and telephone numbers and addresses if we knew them — of all Sally's friends. Of course Conor didn't know any of their names and I only knew a few. Sally had hung around with new friends since Mammy died, and they didn't really talk much whenever I met them. They just stood and looked bored and chewed gum, and sometimes they smoked.

"They all wear black," said Conor. "They're Goths or something like that. What's the one with the stud in her tongue called, Mimi?"

I knew that one because she was Sarah's sister. She looked frightening but she was nicer than her bully sister. "Her name is Tara Sinclair. I know her sister. She lives at fifty-six Bayside Close. But that's the only one I know," I told Aunt M., but she said that was fine. Tara would know the names of the other friends.

"We should stay at home and help look for Sally," said Conor.

"We'll let you know if there's any news," replied Aunt M., not really answering him. "There's no point in everyone getting their knickers in a twist," she said with a grin, and squeezed Conor's knee.

That was just like Aunt M. If you were on a sinking ship, like the *Titanic,* she would say something to make you smile and take your mind off things. "A lot worse things than Sally going missing for a few hours have happened on *Southsiders,* haven't they, Mimi?"

I knew she was just trying to cheer me up—and it did make me feel better when she said things like that.

She dropped off Conor first. I was late again, so Aunt M. came into the school with me and talked outside the door with Ms. Hardy for about ten minutes. When she came in, Ms. Hardy just smiled at me and said nothing—but I could see Sarah making her narrow eyes, and I knew that there would be trouble at recess.

However, at recess Ms. Hardy asked me to stay

back. When everyone had gone out, she called me up to her desk.

I thought I was in for it. "I meant to get my homework done, Ms. Hardy," I blurted out in a rush. "I was in the middle of math when Mrs. Lemon rang the doorbell —"

"Shh!" said Ms. Hardy in a kind voice. "That's not what I want to talk to you about, Mimi."

"Oh," I said, but I could feel this stupid lump in my throat, and I knew if I said anything at all I would just start crying.

"Cry if you feel like it," said Ms. Hardy in such a gentle voice that the next thing I knew I was hugging her and crying and crying, and she was rocking me gently to and fro and whispering, "Shh! There now, there now."

In the end I stopped crying. My face felt all wet and snotty. Ms. Hardy handed me a tissue and I blew my nose like a foghorn.

"Mimi," said Ms. Hardy, in her normal voice, "don't worry about your homework until your sister shows up. You know, she's probably at home right now having a cup of tea," she finished with a smile. "Now, run along before you miss all of your break." And she shooed me out of the room.

Chapter 25

Ms. Hardy was wrong. Sally was not at home when I got back after school. Grandad and Granny were sitting in the kitchen drinking tea.

"Well, if it isn't young Mimi herself," declared Grandad when I walked in, but I could hear in his voice that he was only trying to be cheerful.

"Now, Mimi," said Granny in her bossy voice, "I want you to sit down and drink this lovely hot soup I've made!"

So I drank my soup. Granny and Grandad just sat and watched me. It isn't easy to drink soup when you are being watched. When I slurped it seemed very loud, and soup kept dribbling down my chin. Granny handed me a napkin. I just wished they would behave normally and fuss about. The silence seemed to stretch on and on like an elastic band until I was sure that it would snap. I could even hear a door closing next door. It was weird.

"How was school?" asked Grandad in the end.

"OK," I answered, and then it was silent again.

So I was really glad when my phone beeped. Granny and Grandad jumped.

"Is that Sally?" said Granny before I could even get the phone out of my pocket.

But it wasn't. It was Orla. I heard bt Sal. B der in an hr.

"Read it out," said Granny.

"Only if you want to," added Grandad.

Well, I didn't mind. "It's from Orla. She's heard about Sally and she's coming over in an hour. I don't know why."

"Oh, is that all," said Granny, sounding disappointed.

"It's nice of her," said Grandad. "You know who your friends are when you have troubles." He squeezed my shoulder.

Then the key turned in the front door and we all jumped up. It was Dad and Aunt B. and Aunt M. They didn't look very cheerful.

Dad slumped onto a chair. "Hi, Mimi," he said, and

held out his hand to me. I went over to him and he curled his arm around me and gave me a little hug, and I can't explain why but that made me feel like crying again. But I didn't this time. Aunt M. was talking.

"So I spoke to Tara Sinclair, Sally's friend, and she gave me the names of some of her other friends, and I've spoken to them too and Sally hasn't been in touch with any of them. They had no idea where she might be, but I gave them my number and if they hear anything they'll be in touch straightaway. It seems she has turned off her phone, or maybe the battery is dead. Is it time we called the police?"

I could feel Dad stiffening when she said that.

"I think we should, Paul," said Aunt B.

I remember when the policeman came to our house after Mammy had been run over. He had his cap in his hand and he looked really uncomfortable. I didn't know why he was there. I thought maybe Conor had done something wrong, but Dad just went white and stood back to let the policeman come in. Then he said he had some very bad news about Poppy, and Dad just sort of fell into the armchair and covered his face with his hands and cried, "No, no." Then the policeman put his hand on Dad's shoulder and said that there had been an accident — and that was the worst day of my life.

"I don't want you to tell the policeman," I whimpered.

"I think we have to," said Dad.

"Just wait," I cried. And I pulled out of his arm and ran out of the room and up the stairs and into Sally's room.

Suddenly I knew what I had to do. I knew my sister, and I knew what she would do! So I pulled up her mattress, and without taking one bit of care I pulled out her diary. Then I sat on the floor and flicked through it to the last page of writing, and I was right.

Chapter 26

Dear Mimi,
I just knew you were the spy! And I was right wasn't I?

"How did she guess?" I asked the diary out loud, but of course I got no answer.

So now you know my terrible secret and I suppose you hate me too.

"No, I don't!" I told the diary.

I'm a thief. I steal stuff from nice lovely

Kind Mrs. Lemon of all people. I don't even know why I do it. Since Mammy died I sometimes feel so bad and then I take something and that makes me feel better for a while, but then I feel worse than ever and I will surely end up in jail and that will serve me right.

But at least I don't read other people's diaries, Mimi. Ha!

"It's not as bad as stealing!" I said crossly, because I did feel bad about it but I wasn't going to admit it to Sally. Not that she could hear me.

I'm just teasing you, Mimi! You are my favorite sister in the whole wide world.

"I'm her *only* sister in the whole wide world," I told the diary—but I did like reading it.

And I love you and I even love Conor although I can't stand him most of the time, and I love Daddy and even though everybody hates me now I want you to tell them that I'm OK and that I'm safe and sound and that I haven't gone away forever. Just until

I sort things out in my head a bit—and there is no need to call the police or get into a panic, and I'm sorry to worry everybody because I know they love me, and I will never ever steal again. Tell them that, Mimi . . . and stop reading my diary!

The page was all wet and smudged. Sally must have been blubbering away when she wrote that.

Chapter 27

Everybody turned and looked at me when I walked back into the kitchen. They were all standing or sitting just where they had been when I had run out. It was as if they had all been frozen in time, and now when I walked back in they all started again and Aunt M. asked me if I was all right now.

"Sally is OK," I blurted out. "She says don't call the police."

Everyone looked startled for a moment, and then they all started asking questions.

"Were you talking to her?" asked Dad very quickly.

"Where is she?" said Granny.

"How do you know this?" Aunt B. wanted to know.

"Give the child a chance!" said Grandad to them all.

I took a big breath. I didn't really want to say how I knew, so I said, "She wrote me a note and said that she is OK and don't call the police."

I thought that would stop the questions—but it only made things worse!

"What note?"

"When did you get this?"

"What exactly did the note say?"

"Did she say she was coming back?"

Grandad had to come to my rescue again. "Stop, the lot of you," he said. It was funny to hear Grandad being the bossy one for a change. "Mimi will tell us everything she knows if you give her half a chance."

And that did shut them up. Then Dad asked me gently, "Can you show us the note, Mimi?"

That was the one thing I really did not want to do. "No," I said.

"Oh, for heaven's sake!" snapped Granny. "Her sister has run away from home and we are all worried sick and she won't show us the damn note!"

Granny sounded so cross. She was talking about me as if I weren't there, and I didn't like it one bit. I could feel a lump in my throat.

Then Dad pulled me toward him and sat me on his knee. "Shush," he said to Granny. Granny didn't like that, I could tell. She pursed her lips and looked as though she was about to explode. Then he said to me, "Now, lovey, why can't you show us the note? Did Sally ask you not to?"

"I read it in her diary," I said in a low voice, and I had to look at my shoes. It was my turn to feel ashamed now.

Aunt M. crouched down beside me and took my hand. I couldn't look at her, but there was a smile in her voice when she spoke. "Well, isn't that funny, Sally writing a diary — because the only other person I know who did that was your mother, Poppy. And I know that, Mimi, because I used to secretly read it!"

I could hardly believe it. Aunt M. used to read my mammy's diary. Just like me and Sally.

"Someday I'll tell you what she used to write in it," continued Aunt M.

"Look, I'm sorry for being impatient with you," interrupted Granny, "but I should think, in the circumstances, that you could show us the diary."

"No," said Dad, and Granny threw her eyes to heaven. "I don't think Sally would like Mimi to do that."

"Will you have some sense, for God's sake!" Granny was shouting now. "I've already lost a daughter — I don't want to lose a granddaughter!"

And the next thing Granny was crying in our kitchen and Grandad had his arms around her and was whispering and tut-tutting, “Sally is going to be all right, you’ll see. She’ll be home soon.” He handed her a tissue. Daddy said to me, “Mimi, could you just write down the bit that Sally wrote about being all right. Then we won’t be prying.”

“Please do that, Mimi,” sniffled Granny in the saddest voice. I didn’t say anything. I just slipped off Dad’s knee and went out of the kitchen and up the stairs and started writing down the bit from Sally’s diary that they wanted to see.

Chapter 28

When I came down, Conor was there and so were Emmett and Emma. They must have come in when I was upstairs. Granny was putting out bowls of soup for all of them. Aunt B. was helping her. The kitchen was really crowded. I handed the note to Dad. He read it quietly, then handed it to Aunt B. and she read it out loud. At "*there is no need to call the police,*" the doorbell rang. At first I thought that it was the police, and then Grandad said, "I bet that's your friend Orla."

He was right, and I was glad to go up to my room with her, and Emma came up too while the adults talked about the note.

Orla and Emma had never met, but you wouldn't have known it.

"Are you Dig?" asked Orla.

"No, I'm Dag," answered Emma. "This silly moo is Dig." And she pushed me onto the bed and the next thing, I don't know how it happened, both Emma and Orla were on top of me and tickling me to death, and Emma was telling Orla to watch out "because Mimi does cracker-bums if she gets too giddy!"

And of course I did get too giddy and let out a huge cracker-bum, and both Emma and Orla fell back onto the floor, holding their noses and laughing.

It didn't really seem right to be having so much fun when Sally was missing, but it is hard to be too serious with a friend like Orla and a cousin like Emma.

But then all of a sudden Orla did get serious. "I have a plan for finding Sally," she said.

"Seriously?" asked Emma. She had stopped laughing now too.

"Seriously," said Orla and we all sat on the bed and she explained. "We use Sparkler to track her down. Dogs have a great sense of smell. The police often use them to track down criminals."

"Sally is not a criminal," I said, but then I remembered about the stealing and I realized that she probably was one.

“They use dogs for tracking down missing people as well,” continued Orla.

“That’s right,” said Emma. “The dog gets the scent from a piece of the missing person’s clothes. I saw it on the telly.”

Then I remembered I had seen it too! On *Southsiders* when the old woman with the althesizers, or something like that . . . anyway, she had lost her memory and gotten lost, and they tracked her down with police dogs. The dogs sniffed her cardigan or something. “I’ll get one of Sally’s tops for Sparkler to sniff,” I said, and jumped up.

“Get one that hasn’t been washed,” called Orla. “It will have a stronger smell.”

Emma looked at Orla. “You’re clever!” she said to her, and Orla grinned.

“We’re taking Sparkler for a walk,” I told the adults.

“Taking the dog for a walk?” said Dad, looking puzzled.

“Good idea!” said Aunt B. “Good for the dog and good for you girls. No point in everyone moping around the house all day. Off you go. Chop-chop!”

Well, if Dad was surprised that I was taking Sparkler for a walk, it was nothing compared to how surprised Sparkler was. She charged in the minute I called out,

"Walkies!" and flew around the kitchen, her tail wagging so hard it shook her whole fat body. She knocked into everyone and jumped on Aunt M. and put dirty paws all over her white jeans, and Aunt M. wasn't a bit pleased but everybody smiled in spite of being so sad.

Chapter 29

Once outside the front door, Sparkler made a run for the gate. I was holding on to her lead, but she just dragged me after her.

"She hasn't had a walk for a long time, has she," said Orla as she tried to hold Sally's top up to Sparkler's nose—but Sparkler didn't even seem to notice it.

"SIT, SPARKLER!" I shouted, but of course that made no difference. "Grab her collar," shouted Emma, so we both held her by the collar while Orla held up Sally's top. This time, Sparkler at least noticed the top. She thought that it was a great game. She grabbed it in her teeth, and when Orla tried to pull it away the sleeve ripped off.

"Oh, great," I muttered. "Now Sally is going to kill me!"

"Don't worry about that," said Emma. "We won't tell her. We'll just throw the top in the trash when we're done."

Then Orla shouted, "She's got it! Sparkler's got the scent."

Sparkler was now pawing and sniffing at the torn top as if it was the most interesting thing in the whole wide world. Did she smell Sally on it? Then suddenly Sparkler headed off out through the gate, with Emma and me holding the lead, letting ourselves be pulled along after her. She turned right, and keeping her nose close to the wall trotted along as if she knew exactly where to go.

"Go on, Sparkler, lead us straight to Sally," shouted Orla, all excited.

Well, the scent led to the first lamppost, where Sparkler stopped to do a poop. I knew that I should pick it up, but I didn't have a bag, so I didn't.

"Yuck!" said Orla. "Dogs' bottoms should be corked!"

Then Sparkler found the trail again and was off, sniffing at the wall and dragging us along.

Well, it wasn't a straightforward journey that Sparkler led us on: in and out of front yards and around parked cars, and she stopped at every tree to pee.

"Your dog has sprung a leak," said Orla, which made us all laugh.

To tell the truth I didn't believe that Sparkler was going to lead us to Sally. She's a nice dog, but she is a bit of a brainless mutt. I don't think Orla and Emma believed in Sparkler the great sniffer dog either, but at least it felt as if we were doing something, and in some way it took my mind off Sally's having gone missing. It felt more as though she was playing hide-and-seek with us. But still, in the pit of my stomach there was a hard black lump just like I get when I think of Mammy gone forever.

In the end Sparkler led us into a broken shed near the railway. In the corner of the shed was a large crumpled-up sheet of black plastic, and even in the dim light we could all see something moving under it.

"Sally!" whispered Emma, and lifted a corner of the plastic. Sparkler charged into the gap she'd made, pulling the lead out of my hand, and a terrified cat came squealing out the other side, its fur standing up and its tail standing out.

Orla and I screamed as it flew past us as if its tail were on fire. Sparkler—completely covered in the plastic—raced after it, and Emma nearly broke her sides laughing.

"Sparkler is no sniffer dog," said Orla when she had gotten over her fright.

"It was worth a try," said Emma, and we headed for home.

The journey home was slower, because Sparkler was not fit. This time we were dragging her, instead of the other way around.

Outside our house there was a police car. I stopped in my tracks. My knees felt all weak and shaky. Emma noticed because she said, "Are you OK, Mimi? You've gone all white."

"The police are in my house," I barely whispered. Inside my head a voice was saying that Sally was dead, just like Mammy.

"They have probably found Sally," said Orla.

Chapter 30

The policeman in our house had not found Sally, but he still had his cap on, which must mean that at least she was not dead. He was sitting at the kitchen table writing notes while Dad described Sally. Everyone was still there, and Uncle Horace had arrived too so it was even more crowded. Emma and Orla stayed in the hall. Dad looked up when I came in.

"Sally said don't call the police," I told him in an angry voice.

"Horace had already called them," explained Dad quickly. "They were already on their way when you were reading Sally's diary."

Then the policeman turned to me. He had a kind

face. "You must be Mimi," he said. "Your Uncle Horace did the right thing, Mimi. We are just here to help."

Then Granny clapped her hands and said, "Now, Mimi, why don't you come and stay with me and Grandad for the night? Emma and your friend Orla, if she wants, can come for tea and Grandad can drop them home later. Conor says he wants to stay here with your daddy and help in the search, but you would be happier in my house for one night, wouldn't you?"

I looked at Dad, but he just smiled and said that was a great idea so that was that. I was glad. I really didn't want to stay in our house if Sally wasn't there.

As soon as we got to Granny and Grandad's house, Granny sat us down for cakes and lemonade.

"Our granny makes great cakes, Orla," said Emma while we waited for Granny to get the tea ready.

"Mimi," said Grandad very seriously, "I have some bad news." I must have looked frightened, because he said quickly, "No, no, no, not *that* kind of bad news — just about chess."

"About chess?" I said slowly. I couldn't imagine bad news about chess except if he was going to say that I had to play it now.

"Well, you know your Uncle Horace's computer?" Grandad began.

"Oh, he's always playing on that," interrupted Emma.

"Yeah, so does my dad on his," agreed Orla.

"Well, anyway," continued Grandad, "I got Horace to goggle the origins of chess for me."

"I think you mean Google," said Orla.

"Goggle, Google, what's the difference?" wondered Grandad, shaking his head.

"There's a big difference!" said Emma.

"He's just an old fool," Granny said, laughing as she came in with a tray full of nice things to eat.

"Can I finish my story, please?" asked Grandad, pretending to be annoyed. "Anyway, Mimi, according to Horace's computer, chess was probably invented in India—not in China after all. Now isn't that bad news?"

"That's terrible, Grandad!" I said, and pretended to be horrified. Emma and Orla got a fit of the giggles.

"Of course I can still teach it to you if you like, but it's not really a Chinese game. Are you heartbroken, Mimi?"

"If chess is not Chinese, I don't want to learn it," I said as sadly as I could, while Emma held her sides and fell off her chair.

"So we'll just have to watch boring old *Southsiders* instead!" finished Grandad, shaking his head sadly.

Granny had now set the table and was pouring out lemonade. “Rightio!” she said. “Up off the floor, you, you silly-billy,” she told Emma, “and tuck in.”

“Thank you very much,” said Orla politely. My mouth was already full.

“You are very welcome, young lady,” smiled Granny. “And I’m sorry there aren’t as many éclairs as I thought. I don’t know what’s happened to them. I’ve looked everywhere.”

While Granny was saying this, Grandad was making faces behind her back. He was blowing out his cheeks and sticking out his tummy and pointing at Granny and miming the words, “She ate them.” Emma was drinking lemonade and it all squirted out of her nose when she saw what Grandad was up to. Orla couldn’t keep her giggles in when Emma did that. Giggles are normally very catching, but although I was smiling I just couldn’t seem to catch the giggles today.

“What are you up to behind my back, old man?” asked Granny, and popped an éclair into her mouth, which only made Emma laugh harder.

“Nothing, love,” said Grandad, and winked at me.

Chapter 31

It was quite late when Uncle Horace came for Emma and Orla. He said that there was no news of Sally yet, but the police were keeping a lookout and they all had a copy of her photo and that she was sure to turn up soon. Then he shook my hand and nearly broke my fingers and told me to get some sleep and said that everything looks better in the morning.

I was very tired, and I fell asleep the minute Granny left the room, after giving me a special good-night kiss. Grandad had already rubbed noses with me downstairs and said, "Good-night, sleep tight, and don't let the fleas bite."

Granny had told me to wake her if I felt upset during the night, and promised that "All's well that ends well" and that Sally would definitely turn up soon so I wasn't to worry.

I was too tired to worry anymore. I just fell asleep.

I had a bad dream about Sally. In the dream she was locked outside our house and she could not get in. All the doors were locked, and she kept knocking and knocking at the window. No one could hear her except me, and I was trying to tell Dad. He wouldn't believe me and just kept on watching TV. The knocking was getting louder and louder, and Sally was pushing her face all squashy against the window and shouting, but only I could hear her and see it. "There's nobody there," said Dad, looking right out of the window at her. Then he began to close the curtains, and I tried to stop him. Suddenly Sarah was in my dream, putting on her mocking voice, "There's nobody there, Crybaby. You're all alone." And the knocking was getting louder and louder . . . and it woke me up.

I sat up in bed, breathing very fast, my heart racing. *It was just a dream, Mimi,* I told myself. I wished I had remembered to bring Socky with me.

Then I heard the knocking again. I was awake now, and there it was again. A knock on my window — and then a louder one. I pulled the blanket over my head but the knocking did not go away. *Knock, knock, knock* on my window.

I climbed out of bed, pushed my feet into my slippers, and tiptoed to the window. *Knock* again. I was afraid to open the curtains. I thought about fetching Granny and Grandad, but they were old and they might have heart attacks. *Knock* again. There was nothing for it. I had to pull open those curtains myself.

It could be a hobgoblin. I had been told once about hobgoblins stealing your soul and bashing in your brains. Well, that's what Conor said, anyway. It was a bright sunny day when he told me that, and I hadn't believed a word of it, but now it was dark night and there was a knocking on the window and I just knew that there was a hobgoblin outside. Maybe more than one.

I grabbed the curtains in my fists and counted to three, then yanked them open and jumped back—which was a good thing because a stone came right through the window, smashing the glass all over the carpet.

"Oh, God, now I've gone and done it!" said a voice from the garden. Sally's voice!

I ran to the broken window and looked out. There was a big moon shining all silvery over the garden, and I could see Sally looking up at me. "Sal—" I started to say.

She put her finger to her lips and hissed, "Shush! Don't wake Granny!"

"What are you doing in the garden?" I whispered as loudly as I dared. If the broken window hadn't woken Granny and Grandad, nothing would.

"Trying to wake you up!" whispered Sally back. "I've been throwing pebbles at your window for ages! You're completely deaf, you know!"

"That wasn't a pebble—that was a rock!"

"Yeah, well, whatever. At least you're awake at last. Now sneak downstairs and open the back door," Sally hissed. "I'm freezing out here!"

Chapter 32

My grandparents could sleep through an earthquake. Every step on their stairs squeaked as I sneaked downstairs, but they didn't stir. The back door had about four locks to pull back, and every one of them squealed.

"Hurry up, Mimi!" Sally whispered loudly, hopping up and down on the step.

When I did pull open the door, she jumped inside and gave me a big hug and I gave her a big hug back, and it was as if she had been gone for years instead of just one night and a half.

Then she went straight to the fridge. "I'm famished," she said. "I've only had a few éclairs to eat since I left." She found a cooked chicken leg and started munching it like a starving animal.

"Where were you?" I asked. "Everybody has been looking all over for you. Even Sparkler."

"Sparkler?" Sally had finished the chicken leg and was rooting in the fridge for something else.

"Well, sort of. She found a cat." I decided not to mention her black top. I didn't want her to get mad. "Anyway, where were you hiding?"

"In Grandad's shed!" said Sally, as if it was obvious. She had taken milk out of the fridge and was drinking it straight from the carton.

"Is that so, young lady?" said Grandad's voice—and the kitchen light flicked on.

I jumped and Sally dropped the carton. Milk ran all over the kitchen floor. Maybe my grandparents wouldn't sleep through an earthquake after all. At least not Grandad. He was standing in the doorway in his dressing gown, and his white hair was all standing up. He looked very old. Sally had grabbed a dishcloth and was trying to wipe up the spilled milk. She wouldn't look at him.

"Leave it, Sally," he said kindly, "and come over here and give your old Grandad a hug. Have you any idea how worried we've been about you?"

Sally stood up and handed me the dripping dishcloth. Grandad wrapped her up in his arms like a doll, and Sally just blubbed away on his shoulder as though her heart was broken.

He stroked her hair and said, "Now, now, everything is going to be all right now," over and over, and then he looked up and smiled at me — and, of course, I started crying too. "Come on, you," said Grandad, opening one arm for me, "there's room in these arms for two."

"Group hug," sniffled Sally as the three of us stood hugging and rocking in the kitchen.

I didn't even notice Granny coming in, until she said, "Can I join in?" which made us all laugh.

Sally got a fright when Granny said that even the police were looking for her.

"Are they going to arrest me?" she asked.

"Don't be a nincompoop," said Grandad. "They were just out looking for you like everyone else. Nobody is going to be arrested!"

Sally looked at me then with a question in her eyes.

"I told them what you wrote in your diary about the police," I blurted out in a rush, "but Uncle Horace had already called them. It wasn't my fault!"

"I knew it was you — spy," said Sally, but she was smiling when she said it.

All the same, I could feel myself going red under my skin.

"Now we'd better call your dad," said Grandad. "The poor man is sick with worry."

"It's four in the morning," said Sally. "Let him sleep. We'll call him when he wakes up."

"I very much doubt if he's asleep," replied Grandad. "I'm calling him now."

Grandad was right. He had to call Dad on his mobile because he was out driving around the streets with Conor, looking for Sally. I think Sally was shocked when she heard that. Dad was at the house in less than ten minutes, and when Granny opened the door he just rushed past her and grabbed Sally into his arms and squeezed her tight. He looked like a wild man; his eyes were all black and his hair was a mess and Sally was blubbing again.

Conor just stood there looking at his feet. He doesn't like hugs and that kind of thing. I don't think he knew where to look. "Hi," he said to Sally when Dad let her go, but he looked cross.

"Hi, brother," said Sally, and gave him a quick hug too. It looked funny with Conor's arms straight by his sides and his face red.

* * *

Granny made a big pot of tea, and everyone sat around the kitchen table. "I don't think there's going to be a lot more sleep done around here tonight." She smiled as she poured the tea.

Then Conor just blurted out in a really angry voice, "How could you steal from Mrs. Lemon?"

Sally looked up and her face kind of crumpled and tears started running down her cheeks. Granny stopped pouring tea in midair, and Dad put his arm around Sally and gave Conor a look. "Now's not the time, Conor," he said.

But Sally just looked straight at him and said so quietly that it was hard to hear her, "Because I'm a bad person, Conor."

Conor didn't say anything then. Nobody did for a few seconds. Then Granny said, "That's nonsense."

And Daddy said, "Don't be silly."

And Grandad said, "Why do you think that, Sally?"

Granny wasn't happy about that. She put down the teapot with a bang and frowned at Grandad.

But Sally was looking straight at Grandad and everyone was just waiting, frozen like in a photo, and the room was so quiet that the hum of the fridge seemed loud. Then Sally did a big sniff and whispered in a hoarse kind of voice, "I was the last person to see Mammy before she died."

"We know that, love," said Dad in a gentle voice.

On that Saturday I was playing in the tree house, and I don't know where everyone else was when Mammy left on the bike.

"We were having a fight," continued Sally. Tears were spilling silently down her face. "Well, I was fighting with Mammy. She wasn't taking it very seriously."

"What about?" asked Grandad, and put his hand on top of Sally's hand.

"I wanted a stud in my nose and Mammy wouldn't let me," Sally said in a half laugh, and wiped the back of her other hand across her snotty nose.

"And rightly so!" said Granny. "Disgusting things, those nose studs."

"Anyway, I got mad and—and—" And now Sally got really upset and she pulled her hand back from Grandad's and covered her face, and her voice got loud and all cracked, and I started crying a bit too, and then she said that she had shouted at Mammy that she hated her, and that was the last thing she said to Mammy before she left the house and got run over. And now did Conor see what a bad person she was? Then Sally threw her head down on her arms and cried and cried.

For a long time there was silence around the table, just Sally weeping and Daddy rubbing her back in circles, and then after a long time Grandad said, "And what was the last thing your mammy said to you?"

I wished he'd just be quiet and stop asking these terrible questions, and I think I wasn't the only one because even Daddy looked funnily at him—but Sally lifted her head and, in the saddest voice, said, "Well, you know Mum." She sniffled in a bit of a funny way and she wasn't crying so hard now. "Mammy just laughed and shouted back at me, 'And I love you too, daughter!' and then she blew me a kiss and went. That made me even madder," said Sally with a sort of half laugh and half cry.

"She had already forgiven you," said Grandad in a soft voice, and smiled. "Now blow your nose, child."

Granny pulled a tissue out of her sleeve and handed it to Sally, and she blew her nose like a trumpet.

"So, spy," Sally turned to me, "now you know all my 'dark secrets.'"

Everyone looked at me then, as if it was my turn to say something.

"Nose studs get all snotty," I said. "I'm glad you didn't get one."

And then everyone laughed, even Sally. . . . Even Conor.

"You said what you said with your head, love, not with your heart—so it doesn't count," said Dad.

And Conor told Sally that she wasn't bad, just bad-tempered, and Granny made a fresh pot of tea because nobody had drunk theirs, and she managed to find some éclairs from somewhere that Sally hadn't eaten, and Grandad joked that the woman was impossible and she was obviously stashing away cakes now and no wonder she was so fat! And even Granny laughed.

Chapter 33

The next day in school I was very tired. Dad had said that I could stay in bed because of the long night, but I went to school anyway. By recess I felt so sleepy that I just wanted to fall into a bed.

I get cranky when I'm tired. Maybe if Sarah had known that she would have left me alone, but she just could not keep away.

"Here they come," sighed Orla as the big bully and her lapdogs walked across the yard toward us.

"Hi, Specs. Hi, Crybaby," she called before she even reached us.

I looked at the ground. Orla, of course, looked Sarah straight in the eye. I wished I was as brave as her.

"So, Crybaby, smile!" she jeered. "Your sister is back home again!"

"Go away," Orla growled.

"Ah, don't be like that, Specs," Sarah said in a hurt tone. "We're only here to cheer up poor sad little Crybaby. Isn't that right, girls? So sad since her mammy died."

When Sarah mentioned my mammy and the girls around her laughed uncomfortably, I felt my jaw tighten and a feeling of hate filled me inside.

"I don't know why you are so sad, Crybaby. It wasn't as if she was your real mother, was it?" continued Sarah.

Suddenly there was silence. A really deep silence in the school yard. The other girls didn't laugh. Even Sarah fell silent. Maybe even she knew that she had gone one step too far this time. There was a buzzing in my ears, and for a moment I seemed to be up in the sky, outside my body, looking down on the group of girls in the school yard. Orla and me standing surrounded by the other girls. Sarah standing over me. Ms. Hardy at the top of the steps, stopping and looking across at us, sensing that something had happened . . . or was about to happen.

Then I exploded. "WHAT? WHAT DID YOU JUST SAY?" I roared, louder than I have ever roared before.

I stepped right up to Sarah so my face was an inch from hers, and she stepped back—but I stepped forward again. There was a monster inside me, and it was not going to stay inside! My eyes were burning into Sarah's and she didn't know where to look—she just kept stepping backward, but she could not get away.

All the children in the school yard were paying attention now. All the games stopped. Ms. Hardy was coming down the steps.

"YOU ARE A BULLY, SARAH SINCLAIR, AND YOU ARE ONLY HAPPY WHEN YOU CAN MAKE OTHER PEOPLE MISERABLE! YOU ARE A WORM AND YOU'D JUST BETTER CRAWL BACK INTO THE GROUND BECAUSE IF YOU EVER EVER SAY ANOTHER NASTY EVIL WORD ABOUT ME OR ABOUT MY MOTHER OR ABOUT MY FRIEND I WILL KILL YOU!"

Sarah was backing away fast now. Children were moving aside to let her through, but I wasn't letting her get away. Both my hands were tight fists and I was just about to punch her hard on her big pointy nose when Ms. Hardy grabbed me and held me back.

"OK, everybody, the show is over!" she shouted at the other children. "Go back and play!"

Sarah didn't need to be told twice. She turned and ran! I tried to go after her, but Ms. Hardy is strong and she held me back.

"Cool it, Mimi. Cool it," she was saying as she held me, and there was a little bit of laughter in her voice. "I think Sarah gets the message!"

But I was still boiling over and I struggled to get free.

"Deep breaths, Mimi, deep breaths."

This time I did what she said and took some deep breaths, and slowly I felt myself calming down a bit and fitting back into my body again. Orla was standing in front of me, her mouth open.

"Feeling better now?" Ms. Hardy asked. By now she had half-carried, half-walked me up to the top of the steps. Despite what she had said, a lot of curious children had followed us. . . . But there was no sign of Sarah.

"Yes!" I said. "I'm feeling MUCH better now!"

Ms. Hardy laughed out loud when I said that.

"But I'm not saying sorry!" I told her—and I meant it.

"You most certainly are not," said Ms. Hardy, but quietly this time so that only I and maybe Orla, who was right beside us, could hear. Then she whispered, "I'm proud of you, Mimi. Be proud of yourself."

And that was the first time that I felt really glad that Ms. Hardy was my teacher and not Ms. Addle.

* * *

But I nearly changed my mind again when Ms. Hardy told me before I went home that she would give me detention if I did not do my homework every day from now on.

So I do . . . and it isn't so bad, except for math. I just hate math.

Chapter 34

Homework isn't the only thing changing in our house.

Dad is going back to work part-time. Just for the mornings for now so that we won't go bankrupt, he says.

"What does *bankrupt* mean?" I asked him, but he just tweaked my nose and laughed.

"Ask Uncle Horace; he'll enjoy explaining it to you."

And I will have a monthly bus ticket from now on to get me to school on time. So will Sally and Conor. I'm a bit worried that I will oversleep one day and miss the bus, but Sally says that she will drag me out of bed by the hair.

We all sat down and drew up a roster. That's a timetabley thing with jobs for everyone. It was Dad's idea, but I think he stole it from Aunt B. The jobs change around every week. I've got vacuuming this week and walking the dog. Dad says that our home is going to run like a well-oiled machine, shipshape and everything right on time!

Conor rolled his eyes to heaven when Dad said that, but we all agreed to give it a go. Sally says that she gives it one week max. But Dad thinks that if we all do our bit it will work. I hope that he is right, but I've asked Mammy to help out . . . just in case.

Part 2

Six months later

Chapter 35

Thursday, September 22 — two days to go

"The first time Poppy saw your dad he was going out with her best friend, Caroline, and do you know what she said about him in her diary?" Aunt M. told me as she drove along. We were going to pick up Emma first, then Sally.

"You shouldn't have been reading my mammy's diary," I told her, and grinned.

"Well! That's rich, coming from you, of all people!" She pretended to be highly insulted. "I bet you still read Sally's diary whenever you get the chance!"

"I certainly do not!" I said. It was my turn to be insulted.

"You do so," she said, and she squeezed my knee. "Tell the truth."

"I don't read it anymore."

"Yes, you do!" she said, and she squeezed my knee tighter.

"OK, OK . . . sometimes maybe. Now let go of my knee, please!"

"I knew it. I just knew it." She laughed and put her hands back on the wheel. "You can't fool your Aunty Marigold."

"So what did my mammy say about my daddy in her private diary, Aunt M.?"

"She said that he was a long streak of misery with crooked teeth, greasy hair, and a spotty face and she couldn't see what her friend Caroline saw in him at all. It was obvious that she fancied him straightaway!" And the way Aunt M. said that just made me laugh.

Emma was standing on the path and hopped straight in when Aunt M. pulled over. "Hi, M. Hi, Dig," she said. (She just calls Aunt M. "M.")

Today we were going to fetch our dresses. Sally is going to be the bridesmaid, and Emma and I are going to be the bridesmaid's helpers. "More like my slaves," says Sally.

"What's our job exactly, Aunt M.?" I asked.

"Well, you look pretty and carry flowers and generally you are the gofers."

"Gophers?" I wrinkled up my nose and made faces with Emma. "Aren't they the funny little animals that live in the desert?" There was a photo of a gopher in my nature book.

"Not those gophers," said Aunt M. "Go for this! Go for that! That sort of gofers."

"Oooh," said Emma. "You mean slaves, like Sally says?"

Aunt M. laughed and pulled over the car outside Mrs. Lemon's shop. Sally was already waiting. She works in Mrs. Lemon's shop now every Saturday, but today she popped in to help out because she won't be able to on Saturday. At first she worked for free until she had paid off Mrs. Lemon for all the stationery she had stolen, but now she gets paid. But she says she would work for free and that Mrs. Lemon is her best old-person friend. Today she had Spiff bars for us all.

"Not for me, thanks," said Aunt M. "I want to fit into that wedding dress!"

"One Spiff bar won't kill you," joked Sally. "You're beginning to look like a lollipop! A big round head and a body like a stick."

"Well, thanks very much, Sally. I suppose you'd prefer me to look as fat as my mother?"

"Are you calling our granny fat?" asked Emma. "How dare you!"

"She's my mother and I will call her what I like," answered Aunt M. "I'll probably end up looking like her anyway. Most people end up looking like their mothers."

"I won't end up looking like Mammy," I said.

Everyone went a bit quiet in the car when I said that. Then Aunt M. said, "Well, you're already like Poppy in other ways. You're a bit ditzy, like she was."

"And you read other people's diaries," put in Sally quickly.

I was going to tell her that it wasn't Mammy who did that, it was Aunt M., but my phone beeped and it was a joke from Orla.

Hi. Hav u heard dis 1? Why is a marriage like a 3-ring circus? It has an engagement ring, wedding ring, and suffering.

I had to read it out loud, of course, and they all laughed. But I didn't get it. Anyway, we were at the dress shop then, so everybody forgot about it and we piled out of the car, all excited.

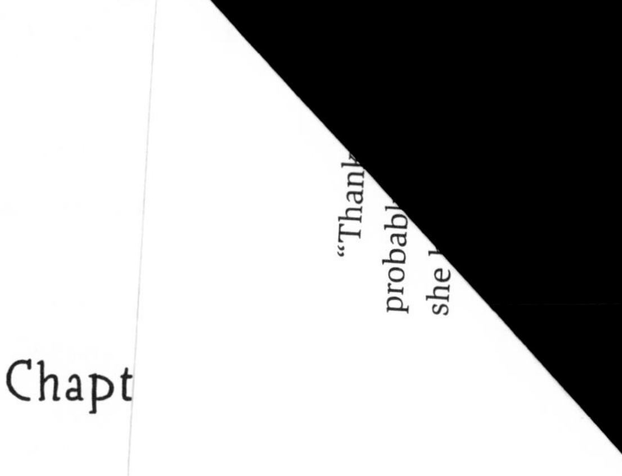

Dad was busy in the kitchen when we all arrived back at the house.

Aunt M. went through to the sunroom at the back to inspect the garden. "The garden looks smashing—but do you think you have planted enough marigolds, Paul?" she called out.

She had a point—our garden was absolutely covered in marigolds, waving their funny orange heads in the wind. We had planted them in honor of Aunt M. for the wedding.

"Damn things sprout like weeds!" answered Dad. "Just like yourself, Marigold."

s for that, Paul," Aunt M. laughed. "Sally
y would have planted lollipops in my honor if
had had her way."

"Now, girls," said Dad to me and Emma, "there's going to be quite a crowd dropping in looking for dinner tonight, so we'd better get cooking. Your fiancé is out with Conor in the shed making a racket," he told Aunt M.

Months ago Nicholas and Aunt M. had asked our family if they could use our back garden for their wedding reception, because it was so big and beautiful and they could not afford the hotel.

I thought they were crazy. "Our garden used to be beautiful," I had said to Aunt M., "when Mammy looked after it. Now it's just a big dog's toilet."

"The grass is up to your waist," Sally added.

"And the bushes are all overgrown and the flowerbeds are probably full of weeds," Conor said.

"Yes. All that is true," Dad agreed. "But, you know, it could be fixed up if we all worked together. We have three months, after all."

"What if it rains on the wedding day?" Sally put in.

"Oh, we thought about that," said Aunt M. "We could put up a tent. Your garden is big enough."

So that's how we ended up having the wedding reception in our garden and it's getting very exciting. It's only two days away. The tent is going up tomorrow.

It was very hard work. Dad did the disgusting bit and cleared up all the dog poop. "That dog is a world champ when it comes to pooing!" he said as he dropped another smelly bag of it into the trash.

Then we had to get going on the lawn—"Hay field, more like!" complained Sally as we chopped away with these big slash hooks Dad rented for the day. Then when it was short enough to cut, we found that the lawn mower had been sitting out in the rain all winter and was rusted away to bits.

"Oh, to hell with it!" said Dad, and threw it in the big Dumpster that he'd rented.

Then—and this is the best bit—Dad bought a riding mower! It's brilliant. You just sit up on it and drive it up and down the garden like a racing driver. We had terrible fights over whose turn it was to cut the grass, until Sally made out a roster so we all get our turn without fighting. Rosters work. . . . Well, most of the time.

"It's ridiculous," said Granny. "Your yard is not that big! Poppy used to cut the lawn with a push mower!"

"You should try it yourself, Gran," said Sally. "It's great fun."

"Oh, I'm much too old for that kind of thing," said Granny, blushing a bit.

"Oh, go on!" urged Grandad, who had already had a go. "You know you want to. Don't worry, it's very strong. You won't break it."

"Go on, Granny," I said.

"Well, if I must," sighed Granny, as if she was doing it just for us. She drove it once around the garden and nearly crashed into a tree.

"Ride 'em, cowboy!" shouted Conor.

It was a good day.

Cleaning the shed out was not a good day.

"Why don't you clear out the shed once and for all, and you can set up your drum kit and have your band practices in there without disturbing all the neighbors," Dad told Conor. "I don't know how often I've said it to you!"

Conor's lips went tight, and he seemed to be bracing himself to do it. He took a few steps toward the shed . . . and then suddenly he turned and ran back into the house and he was crying.

"What's wrong with the boy?" asked Dad in a fed-up kind of voice. "I only told him to clear the shed." He really didn't know what was up. He must have forgotten.

"Do you not remember what's in there, Dad?" said Sally quietly.

Dad stood still for a minute, thinking. "Oh, God," he said. "How could I have forgotten about that? The poor boy." Then he followed Conor into the house, and he was gone for a while.

Sally said, "Leave them to it, Mimi." So we carried on weeding without another word.

Dad came out first. Conor was behind him, but he stopped at the back door and just stood there, watching. He wasn't crying anymore but his eyes were all red. Dad looked really upset but very determined as he strode quickly across to the shed. Sally stood up to follow him, but she took only one step and then stopped.

Dad took a deep breath and pulled open the door of the shed. Through his legs I could see the crumpled-up bike, and suddenly there was this big lump in my throat and my eyes were stinging. Sally was crying softly behind me. Dad stood there for a long time, just looking at the bike. His body looked as tight as a wire, and shivers kept running through him. He had his back to us, so I couldn't see his face. I was glad about that.

Then he made this awful moaning sound that had all the sadness in the world in it, and he bent down and picked up Mammy's crushed bike and carried it quickly down the side passage and out through the front garden and flung it as hard as he could into the

Dumpster. Then he walked back into the yard and stopped and looked at us for a long minute.

"It's gone now," he said in a cracked kind of voice, and his eyes were all red and his face all broken-looking. Then he went slowly back into the house, and when he passed Conor he gave his arm a little squeeze.

I thought I might go after him, but Sally just said, "Give him a minute." So we carried on weeding in silence, and after a bit Conor walked over to the shed and started pulling other stuff out.

After that day it was better in our house.

Chapter 37

"Today we are cooking a popular Italian dish called *spaghetti alla puttanesca*!" declared Dad, kissing his fingers with his lips. "Open the Idiot Book to page nineteen, Mimi."

The Idiot Cookbook was sent to Dad by Aunt L., and it has saved our family from starvation and poisoning.

"It's great," said Emma, poring over the page. "Even a total idiot couldn't go wrong!"

"Thank you, Emma," said Dad. "That makes me feel so good! For that you can chop up the chilies. Make three times as much as it says in the book—we're going to be feeding the hungry hordes tonight."

"That's six chilies, Uncle Paul," she said. "That's going to be hot!"

"Yeah, it is, isn't it?" Dad said with a grin.

I made the spaghetti. The book said 500g of spaghetti and in brackets it read, "For Idiots: 500g is one whole packet." So I had to use three packets, which meant we needed our biggest saucepan.

It was fun cooking with Dad and Emma. Emma really enjoyed the Idiot Book. "Hey, idiot!" she called out. "Is your spaghetti all sticking together?"

"Yes, it is," I said.

"Then put a few drops of olive oil in the water and stir some more. Idiot!"

It seemed a long time ago now that the only food that Dad could make was frozen pizza! (And he couldn't even make that properly.) Now he can even use the washing machine without ruining all the clothes. Aunt B. showed him how to do it right after all of Conor's soccer team's jerseys came out pink.

"My life is ruined!" wailed Conor. "They'll kill me. I can never play football again. I can never show my face again!"

Aunt B. had to sort that out, too. "Oh, don't be so dramatic, Conor," she said in her gruff voice. "I'll dye them red and everyone will be happy. I bet most of your team follow Manchester United or Liverpool anyway, and red is good enough for them." So it all turned out all right.

But Conor isn't the only one who doesn't like pink. "I don't think Sally was too happy with the pink bridesmaid dresses today," said Emma as she stirred the chilies and the garlic in the pan.

Just then the doorbell rang. It was Uncle Horace, who had come to give us our lesson. He was right on time as usual.

Ms. Hardy told Dad that I needed extra help with math because I missed out a lot last year. (Ms. Hardy is still my teacher because Ms. Addle is having another baby. Already. Can you believe that?) So Uncle Horace has said he'll teach me (and Emma, because she's useless at math), if Dad will teach Emmett some chords on the guitar.

"It's a fair swap," said Uncle Horace. "I will shape these young ladies into two of the finest mathematicians this country has ever known, and you can turn my son into a pop star."

So now every Thursday, at half-past five exactly, Uncle Horace arrives with Emma, shakes my hand so hard that my fingers nearly fall off, and then sets about shaping my mind.

"Today we are learning about the most important thing in the world. Money," started Uncle Horace. He had his hands behind his back and was pacing up and down in front of the window.

Outside, Emma and I could see Aunt M. and Nicholas sitting in the yard, their heads nearly touching.

"Money is what makes the world go round." Uncle Horace likes making speeches. "Your Aunt Marigold and young Nicholas wouldn't agree with me right now, but they'll learn soon enough. Love won't pay the bills!"

Emma nudged me. In the yard, Nicholas and Aunt M. had started kissing. She giggled.

"Are you listening to a word I'm saying, Emma?" asked Uncle Horace.

"Of course I am!" replied Emma.

"Then tell me this. What makes the world go round?"

"Love!" answered Emma with a grin.

"Oh, for God's sake!" said Uncle Horace. "You tell her what makes the world go round, Mimi—surely *you've* been listening."

"Love," I said in a dreamy way.

"I give up," said Uncle Horace. "This blooming wedding is turning everyone's brains to mush. We'll have a double lesson instead next week when things return to normal. Now run off, you two scoundrels, and buy yourselves an ice cream or some such tooth rot!"

"Thanks, Uncle Horace," I said, pushing back my chair.

"We've no money," said Emma.

"So what?" laughed Uncle Horace. "You can pay with love!" and he let out a great big guffaw and walked out of the room. But as he was going out of the door he flicked a two-euro coin over his head, and Emma and I nearly broke the table trying to catch it.

Chapter 38

Friday, September 23 — one day to go

At recess Orla had another wedding joke, of course. "This little girl was attending her first wedding—" she started.

"It will be my first wedding too," I interrupted her.

"Mine too. I can't wait," said Orla.

Aunt M. and Nicholas said that Conor and Sally and I can each ask one friend to the wedding because we did such a great job on the yard. Conor is asking his friend from when he was about two, Roger. Sally is asking Tara Sinclair, but she has to promise not to wear black. Sally wanted me to ask Sarah Sinclair so that the two sisters would be there together, but there's no way I'd do that! Sarah and I get on OK now, but she's not exactly my best friend (actually I think she's a little bit afraid of me). Anyway, I'm asking Orla, of course, because she *is* my best friend!

"So, the little girl says to her mother, 'Why is the bride wearing white?'" Orla continued with her joke. "'That's because white is the color of happiness and joy,' explained her mother. 'Then why is the groom wearing black?' asked the girl."

I waited for the next line, but that was it. That was the joke.

"You don't get it, do you," said Orla.

"No. Why does the groom wear black?"

"Oh, Mimi!" groaned Orla, and pretended to pull out her hair. "It isn't that hard to understand! Black is the opposite of white, and so . . ."

But I wasn't listening to her. I was wondering how they were getting on at home.

Not so well, actually. When I got home the tent was up and men were carrying in chairs from a truck parked outside, and Grandad and Nicholas and Dad were hanging the strings of colored lights all around the garden, but inside the tent Aunt M. and Granny were screaming at each other.

"I wouldn't go in there, Mimi," warned Grandad. He was holding the ladder.

"It's World War Three in there, Mimi," added Nicholas from the top of the ladder.

"It's still not too late to change your mind, Nicholas!" joked Dad.

Inside the tent Aunt M. was screaming, "It's *my* wedding and I'll decide where people sit, and Great Aunt Violet can sit on top of a Christmas tree for all I care!"

"I'm just saying—" Granny was talking in her "reasonable" voice, which always made Aunt M. hit the roof.

"I know what you're saying, and I don't give two hoots!" roared Aunt M.

"They say every bride turns into her mother, Nicholas," teased Dad, handing him up a red bulb.

"It sounds as if Marigold already has!" answered Nicholas ruefully.

I decided to go into the house. George was sitting in the kitchen, eating a jam sandwich. George is Nicholas's brother, and he's the best man. Which is a big laugh because George is only sixteen. He isn't even a man. He's a long skinny string bean with hair down past his shoulders. Granny says he's a hippie.

"Hey, man," he said when he saw me. "Want a jam sandwich?"

I looked at the counter. It was covered in crumbs

and lumps of butter and blobs of jam. George is also the biggest slob in the world. "No, thanks," I said, and took a yogurt out of the fridge.

"Cool," said George. Everything is "cool" with George. Granny says the roof could fall in and George would be "cool." "Anyway, I can't talk now, I'm writing my speech." There was a crumpled piece of paper on the counter in among the mess, all scratched-out words and with a streak of jam across it, and George was scratching his head with the chewed-up end of a pen.

"OK, cool," I said and took my yogurt into the sitting room to watch *Southsiders*.

After a little while Aunt M. came in and plonked herself down on the sofa beside me. "Your granny!" she said, but she seemed to have calmed down a bit.

"Is it all sorted out now, Aunt M.?" I asked, one eye still on the telly.

"No, it's not," sighed Aunt M., "but I suppose it will work out on the day. I just hope the good weather keeps up for tomorrow."

"My mammy's in charge of the weather. Dad says it will be fine because she's very reliable."

Aunt M. laughed at that and gave me a little squeeze. "Did you meet the best man?" she asked. It was really hard to follow what was going on in

Southsiders with all Aunt M.'s interruptions. "Nicholas used to be like him when I first met him. A total slob. Your granny thinks he still is!"

"Sally fancies him," I said.

"Who? My Nicholas?"

"No, not your Nicholas," I said. "George!"

"And how do you know that exactly, Miss Mimi?" Aunt M. started poking me in the side with her finger. "Did Sally tell you that?"

"Well . . . not really."

Aunt M. was kneeling on the couch attacking me now, and I couldn't stop laughing. "You read it in her diary, didn't you? Admit it, you little nosy spy! Admit it or die a death by a thousand tickles." We both fell onto the floor then, and between fits of nearly getting sick from laughing I could hear the closing music from *Southsiders.*

In the evening, while it was still bright, Dad and I took Sparkler for her walk. Everyone else had gone home. We walked along quietly, but it was a nice peaceful silence. Then Dad said, "You know that I am going back to work full-time after half-term."

I did know that, but I didn't like to think about it. I didn't like to talk about it either. "Mammy was killed during half-term," I said at last.

"Yes," said Dad. "It doesn't seem like almost a year ago, does it?"

I thought about that. Sometimes it feels as if it happened yesterday, and other times it feels like a hundred years ago. "I wish she was here for the wedding," I said.

"So do I," said Dad, "but we'll have a good day anyway, won't we?" and he put his arm around my shoulder.

"Yes, we will. I can't wait!"

We stopped then because Sparkler had to do her poop, as usual.

When we got back it was dark.

"I want to show you something," said Dad. "Look!"

He flicked a switch and the whole garden lit up like a wonderland with little colored lights all around. It looked magical. And sitting in the middle of the grass, suddenly lit up, were Sally and Conor having a quiet chat.

"Now, off to bed, little miss," said Dad. "You have a big day tomorrow. We all have." And he gave me a special hug.

Before I went to sleep I took Mammy's picture and told her about Sally fancying George, and asked her not to forget to make the sun shine tomorrow, and I told her that I loved her and said good night, sleep tight.

Chapter 39

Saturday, September 24 — the BIG day!

Today lots of good things happened.

First Good Thing: I woke up early and the sun was so bright it was shining right through the curtains. Mammy had done her job.

Second Good Thing: Daddy took Sally and me up to Aunt M.'s apartment to get ready. Emma was already there and the place was a mess. Aunt M. was in a state. Sally had to help her get dressed, and Emma and I had to put on our pink marshmallow dresses, and the phone kept ringing.

"Miss Marigold Roche's residence. Can I be of assistance?" said Emma in a real posh voice when she picked up the phone. It was Granny. "M.—Granny wants to know if you need a hand getting dressed?" Emma called out. "God, no!" Aunt M. muttered under her breath, even though she was a bit worked up. Sally was trying to put her hair up but it looked like a bird's nest. "Tell her no, thanks, everything is fine. Sally has it all in hand!" shouted out Aunt M. from the bedroom.

"Marigold says everything is in order, right on time and shipshape, Granny. Your assistance, while greatly appreciated, will not be required. Thank you and good day." Emma got a fit of the giggles when she put the phone down. "She called me a cheeky little scallywag," she said.

"This isn't working, Sally!" Aunt M. was saying. "I know you're doing your best, but you're clueless!"

"It's just that you won't stand still for a minute!" complained Sally.

"Do you mind if we call Betty?" asked Aunt M.

"Please do!" said Sally, who was getting a bit fed up with it all.

"Emma, call your mother!" shouted Aunt M.

When Aunt Betty arrived, she gave a shake of her head at the state of the place and the state of Aunt M. "Marigold, you are a mess!" she declared, and then she started giving orders.

"Mimi, pick up those clothes and fold them. Sally,

get yourself ready. Emma, keep out of the way. Chop-chop!"

Of course she soon had Aunt M. all dressed and made up and looking like a princess.

"Right, you all look smashing," said Aunt B. "Now can I go home and get ready? I have a wedding to go to!"

"We look like a lollipop and three marshmallows," said Sally, and everyone laughed.

Third Good Thing: Driving to the church with Grandad in the jalopy. Grandad had been polishing up the jalopy for a week now and you could see your face in it. He had tied white ribbons to the trunk and the antenna, and cars hooted at us as we drove by. Emma and Aunt M. and I sat in the back, and Sally sat in the front. Grandad drove very slowly and carefully.

"Keep your hands on the wheel and your eyes on the road, old man!" said Aunt M. in her pretend Granny's voice.

Even though Grandad drove at the speed of a tortoise we got to the church too early—brides are supposed to be late—so Aunt M. made him drive around the block three times.

Fourth Good Thing: Walking up the aisle with Emma, holding Aunt M.'s train (the long tail of her dress), while the wedding music played. Sally had to walk slowly in front, and Aunt M. was holding Grandad's arm and it was just "cool."

Fifth Good Thing: George looked ridiculous in his black suit. It was much too big for him, and every few seconds he had to hitch up the trousers to stop them from falling down. There was a wet patch on the front of his shirt where he had wiped off a spill of jam, and the flower he was wearing seemed to have died.

"He's so cute!" whispered Sally.

George's job was to hand over the wedding rings at the right moment, but he couldn't seem to find them. He searched in all of his pockets. He pulled out a set of keys, a crumpled bunch of paper, which was probably his speech, tissues, a bus ticket, and some euros — which he dropped, and they went rolling down the church.

"Where are they?" hissed Nicholas.

"They're here somewhere, man," whispered George. "Here — hold this."

He handed Nicholas all the stuff he had already taken out of his pockets. Aunt M. turned her head so we could see her face, and she raised her eyes to heaven and a titter went through the church, but I could see out of the corner of my eye that Granny was not a bit pleased.

Then George found the rings at last. "OK, guys, relax — it's cool, I have them," he said, and handed the rings to Nicholas, who handed George back all his rubbish.

Then they put on the rings and Nicholas kissed the bride for about five minutes and then they were married.

Sixth Good Thing: Nicholas was supposed to have rented a big limo to take Aunt M. to the reception in our garden, but he hadn't.

"Oh, Nicholas!" said Aunt M., and everybody thought that they were going to have the first fight of their married life.

But he had a surprise in store. He had a motorbike to take her to the reception—but it wasn't his bike. It was a big shiny black bike with a sidecar sticking out of it. "Ta-da!" he said, and helped Aunt M. into the sidecar. "No need for a helmet. Your hair will stay beautiful." Then he closed the cover over her, and sticking a helmet on his own head he climbed onto the bike and zoomed off down the road.

Everybody cheered, and even Granny had to smile.

"It's just so cool, man," I heard Conor say to George, and it seemed that soon we'd all be talking like George.

Seventh Good Thing: The dinner was good, but it was a bit long; however, the desserts were great. They were all set out on long tables—ice cream, profiteroles, tiramisu, pavlova, chocolate mousse, apple crumbles, blueberries, and all sorts of cakes and chocolates. And the best bit was that you could go up and get more as often as you liked.

"I'll have my work cut out keeping your granny away from that dessert table," whispered Grandad.

"This is the best wedding that I have ever been at," said Orla after she had filled her plate for the fourth time.

"I thought it was the *only* wedding that you had ever been at!" said Emma.

Wee Billy loved the desserts as well. He especially loved putting his hands in them and running away when Aunt L. tried to catch him. He seemed to have taken a liking to George because he kept running after him, and soon George had sticky handprints all over his black suit. Sally told Aunt L. that she would look after wee Billy as soon as she saw that he kept running to George.

"How's my wee lass?" roared Uncle Boris when he saw me, and he swung me up in the air. "Now open your gob and show me all these fillings you've got!" Uncle Boris is a dentist, so he had a good look when I opened my mouth, and when he was done he said, "Good job. Serves you right, of course, never brushing your teeth," and then he swung me in the air again. I think he had drunk too much wine.

Chapter 40

Actually, a lot of good things happened that day — too many for one chapter!

Eighth Good Thing: The speeches. Well, actually, the speeches weren't all good. Some of them were very boring. Grandad's speech was nice but it was a bit mushy. Aunt M. was smiling and crying at the same time when he said that all his daughters were beautiful flowers and, even though she wasn't here today, Poppy's spirit was everywhere to be seen and you only had to look at her beautiful children, Conor, Sally, and Mimi, to understand that. A lot of people had to blow their noses when he said that.

George's speech wasn't mushy at all. When he stood up he looked very nervous and he couldn't say anything for a bit. But then somebody shouted, "Come on, man, get on with it!" and he grinned and uncrumpled the jammy piece of paper that his speech was written on.

"Hi, guys," he started, and gave a little wave. "I just want to welcome Marigold into our family. . . . She's, uh . . ." He had to struggle to find the right word, but it came to him in the end. "She's . . . cool." Everyone clapped then, which gave George a chance to relax a little. "Like . . . uh . . . the old man said . . . she's a flower. . . . " Everyone burst out laughing at that, and Grandad pretended to be upset about being called an old man. "Less of the 'old man,' please!" he called down the table.

"Yeah, right," muttered George. "Sorry, man," and he gave Grandad a kind of thumbs-up.

I could see Granny shaking her head, but she was trying very hard not to smile too.

"Anyway, man, Marigold's a flower and she's marrying my brother and he can be a bit prickly, like a rose . . . so that makes two flowers." George had to stop again because everyone was laughing. When it settled down again he continued, "Anyway . . . that's all I have to say because that crazy dog, Sparks or whatever, ate the other half of my speech. . . . So, anyway, relax. Stay cool. Have a good evening." Then he sat down — but he had to jump up again because he had forgotten to make the toast.

By the way, making the toast doesn't mean making toast — it means drinking.

"A toast to the bride and groom — may they always be two blooming flowers!" George called out, and everyone drank their champagne and shouted out "To the bride and groom!" and Dad put a little champagne in my glass, and the bubbles bounced off my nose when I drank it and it tasted lovely, but Dad wouldn't give me any more.

Ninth Good Thing: The first dance. Nicholas and Aunt M. danced all on their own for a while — it was really slow and smoochy — and then George had to dance with Sally and he wasn't very good. I could hear him saying "Sorry, man" every time he stepped on her toes, but Sally didn't seem to mind at all. Then I had to dance with Emmett, and Emma had to dance with Conor, because we were the bridesmaid's helpers and they were the ushers or something like that. Emmett danced very fast and we fell down twice. I wondered if he had been finishing off what was left in the wine-glasses again.

Tenth Good Thing: After that the band played a

lot of songs and everyone got up to dance. Sally and George danced together every time, and Aunt M. whispered in my ear that she wanted a full report of Sally's diary when she came back from her honeymoon.

Then it was Conor's big moment. Nicholas asked the drummer to give Conor a go. Conor's face was very red as he took the drumsticks, but he soon got into it and started belting away and making a terrible racket. Everybody cheered and the band thought that he was so good they asked him to stay on and play with them for a while.

"Man!" said George. "He's giving it socks! Your brother is so — I don't know — so cool!"

Then they asked if anyone else would like to sing, but that was a big mistake because Great-Aunt Violet tottered up onto the stage and her singing was so awful that Emma got a total fit of the giggles, and I had to put my hand over her mouth to try to keep her quiet — but that only made her laugh more.

The Eleventh Good Thing: It was still hot outside when it got dark, and Dad switched on the strings of colored lights and made the garden look like a magical place. Aunt L. was sitting on a garden bench telling Uncle Horace that we were having a lovely Indian summer this year, which I didn't understand. It was an Irish autumn, wasn't it? Uncle Horace was saying that it was very unseasonable weather and it was a sure sign of global warming—and suddenly I felt very tired.

Aunt B. had taken Emma home, and Orla had left ages ago. Even Aunt M. and Nicholas had gone off to their hotel, and although Dad had said that I could stay up as long as I liked, I now felt so sleepy that all I wanted to do was go to bed.

I found Dad talking to Nicholas's father, and I kissed him good night, and then I found Granny and Grandad just as they were about to leave.

"Your old granny is not up to these late nights anymore," said Grandad, and Granny elbowed him in the ribs.

I gave them both a hug and climbed up the stairs to my bedroom. I had to be very quiet, because wee Billy was asleep in his cot in my room and I didn't want to wake him.

I brushed my teeth for three minutes—well, maybe not the full three minutes—and crawled under my duvet. Socky was already asleep so I didn't disturb him, but I told Mammy's picture that it had been the best day and good night, sleep tight, and somehow it felt like she was right there with me.

And in the distance I could hear the band playing "Perfect Day" as I drifted off to sleep.